By Dean Murray

Reflections

Broken

Torn

Splintered

Intrusion

Numb

Trapped

Forsaken

Riven

Driven

Lost

Marked

Dark Reflections

Bound

Hunted

Ambushed

Shattered

Burned

The Awakening

Reborn

Immortal

Endless

A Broken World

The Society

The Destroyer

The Founder

The Desolation

Reflections
(Dean Writing as Eldon)

The Greater Darkness

A Darkness Mirrored

The Guadel Chronicles

Frozen Prospects

Thawed Fortunes

I'rone

Brittle Bonds

Shattered Ties

Riven

Dean Murray

Copyright © 2013 by Dean Murray

Published by Fir'shan Publishing

ISBN 978-1-9393633-6-7

www.FirshanPublishing.com

First Edition

For all of the authors who entertained and inspired me growing up

Chapter 1

Adriana Page
Graves Estate
Sanctuary, Utah

I had to keep telling myself that my mom flying into town wasn't as scary as seeing Agony nearly kill Alec. My brain knew that this wasn't going to be nearly as bad as what I'd seen almost happen in Chicago, but my emotions kept trying to convince the rest of me that the end of the world was about to take place.

Alec grabbed my hand as I started tapping a nervous beat on my leg for the fifth time since we'd sat down. I started to apologize again for fidgeting, but he simply smiled at me and gave my hand a reassuring squeeze.

"James and Dominic just texted me. Your mom's plane has landed. Knowing the way James drives, your mom will be here in less than ten minutes. Trust me, the anticipation is the worst part. Once your mom is here we'll have a calm discussion and then work everything out."

I gave him a brave nod, but I wasn't convinced, not really. Alec's mom spent most of each day lost in memories of happier times which meant that he'd more or less been raised by Donovan. Donovan was extraordinary, and I'd never been tempted to dismiss him as 'just one of the help,' but there was a different dynamic there than what Alec would have had with a parent who wasn't also the family butler. Donovan had always given Alec an incredible amount of leeway, way more than my mom had ever given me. It meant that Alec didn't really know what he was going to be in for when my mom arrived.

"Okay, I'll try to calm down. Just remember, I want to be with you no matter what. Short of hurting my mom or something like that, we need to keep escalating things until she agrees to let me stay here. It's important."

Alec nodded. "Things will be okay, I promise."

The next few minutes seemed to drag by, but then suddenly I could hear Donovan escorting my mom back to the sitting room where we'd been waiting for the last half hour.

"May I present Mrs. Nicole Paige and Mr. Russ Landsell."

As Donovan bowed and then retreated from the room with only a trace of his normal limp, I tried to adjust to the fact that things were already going a different direction than I'd expected. Mom had only been dating Russ for a few weeks, a couple of months at the max. I never would have expected for Mom to bring him along on a mission to come collect her wayward daughter.

Mom and Russ both took the chairs that Alec offered them, and then sat down slowly. I couldn't read the expression on Mom's face, but both she and Russ seemed content to let Alec start the discussion.

"I appreciate you coming out here, Mrs. Paige, Mr. Landsell. Under other circumstances I would have flown out to you rather than asking you to make the trip, but I'm afraid I'm not able to travel right now."

That was Alec-speak for the fact that the Coun'hij could attack us at any minute. Alec's power had finally fully manifested. That meant he could protect us all as long as he was around, but if he were to fly out to New York it would leave us all vulnerable.

"You didn't exactly leave me any choice. I got a call from my daughter from a blocked number telling me to be on your plane with a date and time."

I winced. A cowardly part of me wanted to just hang back and let Alec take the brunt of the attack, but that wouldn't be fair.

"That's not Alec's fault, Mom. I was the one who insisted on not giving you any more information than that. I didn't want to risk you causing him problems."

Mom looked at me for the first time, I mean really looked, and I saw just how mad she was. "Do you have any idea how worried I've been, Adri? First your school calls to tell me that you weren't in classes and then you didn't answer your phone when I called."

"I'm sorry, Mom. I didn't mean to make you worry, but I needed to be here."

"You needed to be here? Adri, this is the place that you just left. We talked and you agreed that Alec needed a wakeup call. You left here for a reason."

I fought a rising tide of anger and forced my voice to remain even. "Yes, Mom. I left for a reason and I came back for a reason. Alec and Rachel need me here right now, and I'm going to stay here."

It looked like my mom was going to start yelling at me, but Russ put a hand on her arm and spoke for the first time.

"Alec, I've been talking to some of my contacts in the FBI. Nicole hasn't filed a police report yet, but once she does it will be routed right to the FBI. You've kidnapped a minor and taken her across state lines. The repercussions are going to be pretty serious."

Alec shook his head. "I haven't kidnapped anyone. Adri left the state of New York without my knowledge. I have a dozen people ready to testify to the fact that Adri came here of her own free will, up to and including the pilot of the plane that brought her here."

"Your pilot. That's hardly a very independent witness, Alec. Trust me, things will go much better if you just back down and let Adri come back to New York with us."

It was like watching two dogs circling each other, looking for a weakness. I almost wanted to think less of my mom for bringing Russ along, but I understood why she had. Neither of us was versed in wealth, not like Russ or Alec were. Mom knew just how much influence Alec had in Sanctuary from when we'd lived here before. Mom couldn't combat that, but there was a chance that Russ could. Besides, it would be pretty hypocritical to look down on Mom for bringing Russ into the picture when I was sitting here hoping that Alec could wave a magic wand and make everything work out with my mom.

The thought served as a goad and I waved my arm at Mom to get her attention. "I know that you don't like it, but I'm determined to stay here and I'm willing to go as far as I have to for that to happen. If you fight me on this then I'll get legally emancipated."

Mom went white and collapsed backwards into her chair like I'd hit her. It was Russ who tried to calm both of us Paige women down.

"Let's not do anything hasty. Adri, I know you and your mom aren't seeing eye to eye right now, but emancipation isn't a trivial thing to pursue. There isn't even any guarantee that you'd win."

Alec looked at me with a question in his eyes, but I nodded so he took a deep breath and responded. "I have a team of lawyers who are very confident they can win the preliminary case, and in fact we've already got feelers out to two of the three judges we think are most likely to try the case, and given the circumstances, they are both in agreement that Adri would win."

Russ' smile wasn't in the slightest bit ruffled. "You're bluffing. Adri has no way of supporting herself. No judge in the world is going to stick their neck out that far. The ruling would be overturned in appeals so fast that everyone involved would get whiplash."

I felt my expression stiffen. Alec and I hadn't gone into those kinds of details. He'd just told me that he'd be able to handle everything and I'd believed him. I turned to ask Alec if Russ was right, but he smiled at me and then picked up a thick stack of papers.

"I rarely bluff, and never about people who matter to me." Alec tossed the folder to Russ and then he gave the other man the kind of cold smile that he usually reserved for the Coun'hij. "The top document is a fully-executed, irrevocable trust with Adri as the beneficiary. I think you'll find the trust assets are more than sufficient to allow Adri to support herself quite nicely until well after she reaches her legal majority. The documents below that detail all of your holdings. I think you'll find it's quite comprehensive."

Russ opened the folder and then spent a few minutes scanning through the documents while my mom and I both shifted nervously in our seats. When Russ finally looked up from the stack of paper there was a new wariness to his posture that hadn't been there when he first arrived.

"Don't you think that ten million dollars was a little excessive, Alec? That kind of wealth could turn her into a spoiled snob who isn't worth the air she breathes. It could destroy her."

My heart skipped a beat. I almost thought that I'd misheard the amount, but my mom's expression told me that I'd heard correctly. Not only had I not known anything about the trust, I would have opposed him putting so much money into it if I'd been aware of what he'd been planning.

Alec waved away Russ' point without missing a beat. "It's got all of the usual provisions designed to guard against that kind of thing. She can't touch the principal until she's twenty-six, and there are even caps on the amount she can draw out in any given year until then. It's the same kind of vehicle that Donovan set up for Rachel, but that's beside the point. I've made the mistake of underestimating Adri's strength too many times already. The wealth won't ruin her any more than it ruined you."

Russ considered the response and then flipped through the second half of the folder again. "Should I take the presence of the rest of this to indicate that you're threatening me?"

"No, nothing of the kind. I merely wanted to provide you with a sense of my capabilities. I think things will go much more smoothly if you understand exactly what you're up against."

Russ frowned and then looked at me. "I can tell this is as much of a surprise to you as it was to me. With this trust you won't ever have to work a day in your life if you don't want to. It means that there isn't any monetary reason for you to stay with Alec."

A flash of anger nearly made me give Russ a piece of my mind, but I stomped on my fury and shook my head at him.

"I thought you knew me better than that, Russ. I'm not here because of Alec's money. I'm here because this is where I'm needed. You could say that I've found my cause, but it's more than that. This is where I'm happy. I'm not some stupid, love-struck teenager. I know what I'm getting into, better actually than either of you do, and this is the future I want."

I hadn't planned on referencing his insight, but hopefully me telling him that Alec was my cause, the person I wanted to enable, would give Russ pause enough for him to actually hear what

I was trying to say rather than just assuming that I was being stupid.

"I see. You're sure that you know what you're doing here?"

I nodded and then waited while he looked over at my mom. "It's your call, Nicole. We can file a report but you'll be in for a long fight one way or another. With a little bit of luck we can make sure she's back in New York while the lawyers bicker, but it isn't guaranteed."

I interrupted before he could continue. "I'll run away. Even if you can keep me away from Alec, I'll still make sure that I'm not home."

Russ winced a little, like he'd been hoping that I wouldn't realize that was an option, and then shrugged. "There are measures we could take, but nothing we could do would guarantee that she'd stay there with you. I'm willing to help you if that's what you want to do, but you need to know what kind of fight you'd be taking on."

Mom looked old. Somehow the stress of her professional commitments had aged her without me realizing it, but it was more than just all of the hours she was putting into work—my disappearing must have been even harder on her than I'd expected. She tapped the arm of her chair for several seconds and then frowned. "So it's going to be expensive."

Russ took her hand in his and squeezed it. "Don't worry about that. If you want to pursue that option I'll have my people take care of things."

Mom shook her head. "No, it's a hopeless cause. I've been gone more than I've been around. There isn't any way that we could win, not given how absent I've been lately."

I was glad that Mom had been the one to point that out. I'd been ready to go there if I had to, but I hadn't wanted to.

Russ sighed. "It will make things more difficult, but you shouldn't make this kind of decision based on fear. The real question is whether or not you think that Adri is mature enough to be on her own. If she is as much of an adult as she thinks she is, then you should trust her when she says that she knows what she's getting into. If not, then we should do whatever we have to in order to get her back."

Mom looked at me for several long seconds, and I could feel the decision balancing on the edge of a knife. Mom hadn't ever been big on tears. Most of the time she was too caught up inside of her head to let sorrow really touch her. She'd only cried once or twice since the funeral. She was crying now though and I was struggling not to join her.

"Okay. You can stay, Adri. I hope you really know what you're getting into, but if it turns out that you get in over your head then I want you to know that you can always come home."

I made it from my chair over to my mom's chair without realizing that I'd crossed the intervening distance. She wrapped her arms around me and for a couple of minutes I just sat in her lap like I'd done when I was little.

"I'm sorry, usually I'm not such a baby. I must look terrible." Mom dabbed futilely at her mascara and then looked around. "Is there a bathroom nearby?"

Alec nodded and stood as if to show her where it was but she waved him back down into his seat. "Just point me in the right direction and I'll be fine."

"It's back out the direction you came in from, down the hall, take your first left and it's the second door on the right."

Once Mom was gone and it was just the three of us, I turned back to Russ and took a deep breath. "What are you going to tell Mom? What have you observed while you've been here?"

Russ leaned back in his chair and gave me a measuring look. "I'm not entirely sure I should be telling you any of that, especially not with Alec in the room. Your mom's decision to let you stay here notwithstanding, I suspect that we're not exactly playing on the same team."

"Please, Russ. I need to know how much you've figured out because it will impact just how much of a problem my mom is going to be in the future."

"I've noticed, I suspect, more than you'd like me to have noticed, but there are still threads there that I can only begin to guess at."

I hadn't told Alec about Russ' ability to read people and situations because it hadn't really been my secret to give up, but he didn't seem at all fazed by the direction of the discussion. Russ met my gaze for several more seconds before finally shrugging.

"Alec obviously isn't your run-of-the-mill billionaire. He's almost more like royalty. Dominic was obviously serving as your bodyguard back in New York, but there is a different feel to things here. It's sort of like the Dark Ages. I don't get the feeling that Alec needs protecting from most threats, but his house seems chock-full of extremely dangerous teenagers. The best description I can give is that Alec is the king and he's surrounded himself with dukes and counts not because he fears any one man, but because he knows he'll need an army at his back if he's to protect his realm."

Alec gave Russ a nod of respect. "That's more insightful than most. I won't insult you by offering you a job that you don't need, but if you are ever in a position where you need a...diversion...I can make it worth your while."

Russ' chuckle gave the impression that he'd just filed away another piece of information in a mental folder somewhere with Alec's name on it.

"Money doesn't mean anything to you, but not because you're some spoiled heir. It's a tool and nothing else, but I get the sense that you just...expanded your reach somehow. With someone else I would say that they'd come into a substantial increase in working capital, but I have the feeling that isn't it. You've got some kind of new tool in your back pocket though."

I fought to keep my expression under control, but I was pretty sure that I didn't succeed. Russ was keying into things that I never would have expected him to catch. I was scared to find out what else he suspected, but it was better to know than remain ignorant.

Russ sighed and then uncrossed his legs and leaned slightly forward. "I can tell that you are head over heels in love with each other, and there is more to that bond than I would have expected. It's almost like you've been through some kind of armed conflict together."

Alec gave Russ another nod and a smile. "You could say that we've been through our own little pocket of hell over the last few months."

"I don't want to know about that. The less I know the less Nicole can tease out of me at some point down the road. Understand this though, Alec. I know firsthand that being in love with someone now doesn't necessarily mean that you'll continue to keep her best interests at heart. If you do something to hurt her—really hurt her, not some stupid lovers' quarrel—then I will kill you. You can probably buy and sell me several times over, but I won't stand by and watch Nicole or Adri be hurt for no reason. You may be just as dangerous as you appear to be, but that won't stop me from taking you out from a mile away if that's the only way to make you pay for your sins."

A flare of power roared out from Alec, and it dwarfed nearly anything I'd ever felt out of him. It was so strong that even Russ seemed to sense the fringes of it. I could almost see the wheels turning in his head as he upped his evaluation of just how dangerous Alec was. Alec got control of his beast with an almost visible effort of will and then nodded at Russ.

"If I proved myself so lost as to hurt Adri in the way you've described, then I would truly deserve the bullet you've just threatened me with. Be very careful though with regards to the threats you choose to level at me. The consequences are likely beyond what you're expecting."

The silence in the room did a poor job of masking the fact that Russ and Alec were sizing each other up with new eyes. Before things could become further strained, Ash entered the room and leaned in so that he could whisper to Alec. Another surge of power lashed out from Alec, but this time it wasn't directed at anyone in the room. Alec debated his course for a second before nodding to himself and then turning back to Russ.

"Ash has just informed me that we've got an unusually large group of cars heading this way. It is likely nothing to be seriously worried about, but given some recent developments, there is the chance that things could get unpleasant. I leave it up to you whether or not you stay or go, but know that if you stay Adri's mother may be exposed to things that you'd rather not have her see."

"What kinds of things?"

"Adri tells me that you're a veteran of the conflicts in the Middle East. The cars on their way here may be planning on bringing that kind of violence here to my home. If you choose to stay I will do everything in my power to protect you both, but there is a very real possibility that I won't be able to keep you completely safe."

Chapter 2

Alec Graves
Graves Estate
Sanctuary, Utah

Russ' eyes had gotten bigger and his heart rate had sped up slightly when I'd told him there was a possibility that he, Adri, and Nicole were all in danger if they remained here, but it was the closest thing to a nonresponse that I'd seen out of a human in a long time.

"Okay, I'll do what I can to get Nicole out of here, but I think that Adri should leave with us. She can come back once the danger has passed."

Adri interrupted before I could get a response out. "I'm not going anywhere. I really do know what I'm getting into, Russ. I'd appreciate it if you could get my mom out of here, she doesn't need to see any of this, but I'll be fine here."

Russ gave Adri a long look, but in the end he nodded and then turned back to me. "Can we take your jet back or do I need to make other arrangements?"

Right to the point. I liked that. "Ash already has one of the planes prepping for takeoff and a helicopter on the way here to take you back to the airport."

"What are the odds that we'll get ambushed at the airport?"

"I think that they'll leave you alone. They won't want to cause big problems out where there are a lot of witnesses. I'll send Dom, Jessica, and Jasmin with you, but I'll need to keep the boys here in case the helicopter doesn't make it back before our visitors arrive."

I could tell that he didn't like that, but it was more than I should have been offering him. My power seemed to be working just fine now, but if, for some reason, it went dormant again then we were going to need every warm body we had to try and stand off any kind of decent-sized attack.

"Okay. Do you have a weapon I can borrow? Presumably you can keep the local authorities from coming down too hard on me, so I'd rather not go unarmed if things are as bad as you're indicating."

I shot Ash an inquiring look and he nodded and pulled a pistol still in a pocket holster out of his pants. Russ accepted the pistol with a low whistle. "A Kimber .45. You don't skimp on your weapons."

Russ ejected the magazine, checked that it was loaded, and then slammed it back home and racked the slide. A second later the weapon vanished into Russ' right front pocket as he heard Nicole approaching. Russ turned towards her and met her with a frown.

"I'm sorry, Nicole. I just got a call from Patrick. It sounds like there is a situation developing with the property purchase we've spent the last six months working on. I hate to tear you away from Adri so soon, but I'm afraid things aren't going to be pretty if I'm not back in New York within the next few hours."

Adri's mother's disappointment was obvious, but there was a hint of something that felt like relief mixed with a little bit of guilt. I spared a moment to wonder whether or not to tell Adri just how ill-equipped her mom felt when it came to dealing with her teenage daughter, and then Nicole and Adri were making their tearful goodbyes.

Ash had already left, presumably to round up the girls so that Russ and Nicole had their escort. Less than ten minutes after Ash had delivered news of the inbound vehicles, Adri and I were watching her mom and Russ take off.

Half an hour later, Jasmin, Dominic and Jess all made it back just as the first of the loose caravan of cars pulled up. There were six in total and Ash had already informed me that they were spread out nearly half an hour apart between the first and the last. It was an unlikely configuration for an attack force, but nobody had called ahead to tell us that they were sending a delegation, so we had to play it safe.

Nobody really knew just how much control Puppeteer could exercise over a werewolf, but if he could stuff those cars even half-full of werewolves then we'd all be dead within minutes of their arrival.

The pack had all gathered out in front of the house. Even most of the non-combatants were there with us. James and Isaac stood slightly behind and to either side of me with Dominic and Jessica at their respective flanks. Jasmin paced back and forth on Dominic's side of the arc while Ash and Kristin anchored the other side of the group.

Rachel, Adri, Donovan, and Andrew all stood on the front step, near enough they could hear what was being said, but far enough away that they were less likely to get pulled into the fringes of the fight if our visitors were hostile. Addison was with my mother, which put her safely out of the way. She'd still do her best to make life difficult for me by putting a bug in James' ear but at least this way she couldn't stir the pot directly.

The first person to step out of a vehicle was a blond guy who was nearly as tall as Isaac and who was actually a couple of inches wider through the shoulders. He looked like he was in his early forties, which probably put him nearly into his third century given how much slower we aged than humans. The blond guy waited just long enough for two women to get out of the SUV and then all three of them walked towards us.

The girls were physically alike enough to each other that I was pretty sure they were sisters. Both were blonde with the kind of stocky frame you'd expect on female boxers. They didn't have any excess fat anywhere on their bodies, but it was obvious that they weren't the kind of girls to take a back seat to a bunch of boys when it came to any kind of physical endeavor.

One of the girls looked like she was about Rachel's age and the other looked like she was in her early twenties. It was almost unheard of for shape shifters to have children that close together. Something about our physiology gave us lower birthrates than humans. It wasn't uncommon for siblings to be a decade apart, more even for weaker shape shifters.

If both of these girls were our new arrival's daughters, then he was making a statement about his probable level of power simply by bringing them here. As the trio made their way over to us, the second vehicle, a black Mercedes, pulled up.

A pair of brunette women got out of the Mercedes. The older one looked like she was getting into her third century, but she was still a powerful figure. The presence of a single, jagged scar across her left cheek told me that she'd had a run-in with Agony at some point. Her companion looked like she was in her late twenties or early thirties, and the two were related unless I was very mistaken.

The big blond guy was nearly to us, so I turned my attention back to him as he stopped in front of me and nodded. "My name is Raynor. I come from the Durango Colorado pack to request guest right from you, Alec Graves."

"You're bold to have come here without calling ahead to ask permission to pay us a visit."

Raynor's smile was challenging. "The rumors of your fight with Agony have already shot across the land like wildfire. They are as varied as they are incredible, but there are two things that they agree on. You killed Agony in a display of power that makes you the equal of almost any of the Coun'hij, and you declared war on the governing body over every wolf in North America. One could say that you're setting yourself up as our new king, Alec. If that's true then you'll remember that the kings of centuries past always allowed their subjects to come and go as they pleased."

"Are you here to swear allegiance to me, Raynor?"

The smile was back. I was very much getting the feeling that Raynor wouldn't ever make a very restful ally. "I think it's too soon for us to talk of such things. Let's say that I've come to explore the possibilities of an alliance. In the meantime, surely someone as powerful as you are doesn't have anything to fear from someone like me."

Fat chance of that. My intel on most of the other packs was still substandard, but Ash and Donovan were working hard to correct that situation. Raynor was an alpha cast from the same mold as Ulrich Bishop. He'd never manifested a power, but he had a larger than average pack which he controlled with a completeness that was nothing less than amazing.

Raynor was tough enough that he could take down most of the rest of his dominants. The few who were tougher than him were controlled via his vast financial resources. If Raynor decided to actively work against me he was capable of causing me no end of headaches.

"Very well, I offer you guest right here in Sanctuary. As long as you aren't working against my interests I'll see to it that you're taken care of and protected to the best of my ability."

I got another nod from Raynor and then he motioned his companions forward. "These are my daughters, Nadine and Bridget. I hope that the three of you will have a chance to get acquainted while we are here."

I should have seen it coming, especially after the situation with Tasha, but he caught me off guard enough that my pulse flickered. The last thing I wanted at this point was a political marriage, but now wasn't the time to tell him that I'd have his alliance without marrying one of his daughters or I wouldn't have his alliance at all.

"I'm sure they are both lovely individuals."

Raynor opened his mouth, probably to press for a firmer commitment out of me, but I turned to the two who'd arrived just after him, preempting whatever he'd been about to say. The older of the two stepped forward and gave me a nod.

"I am Rebekka Jansen from the Tonopah pack. My daughter Vivian and I likewise have come to ask for guest right."

Interesting. Not that the Tonopah Nevada pack had also sent a representative. They were in even worse shape than Jaclyn and Tasha's pack so it actually made a lot of sense for them to play for an alliance with us. No, the interesting thing was that Rebekka didn't want to be offering her daughter up to me as a prospective wife. There was something there I could work with. If I could get past her distrust then there was a chance that I could bind the Tonopah pack very closely to me indeed.

"I welcome you to Sanctuary, Rebekka, Vivian. I extend the same promise to you that I just extended to Raynor. As long as the two of you behave as guests then you'll have the protection of my house to the full extent that I'm able to offer it."

"Thank you, Alec. Will you need help with those other cars?"

I looked up at the road as the third and fourth vehicles came into sight and then shrugged. "None of our visitors today bothered announcing themselves beforehand. I expect that none of them will be a threat, but I would welcome your help until such a time as we've confirmed that none of the other four vehicles are planning on attacking."

Rebekka nodded and then motioned for her daughter to take a place next to Jasmin. Raynor couldn't let her upstage him so he took up a position on the other end of our arc, next to Ash and Kristin.

The next set of arrivals was a quartet of guys who made my beast try to force a transformation. The leader was as big as Brandon had been and he moved like Abaddon. Physical size in human form didn't *always* correlate to size as a hybrid, but it usually did and something told me that this guy was extremely dangerous.

The four of them shook out into a loose diamond formation and then approached me. The leader was scanning through the group that stood next to me as he walked forward. He started with Rebekka and Jasmin and was nearly to the other end before he missed a step.

For a split second I thought that it had been Raynor's presence that had unnerved him, but I was wrong.

"I came here to discuss an alliance with you, Graves, but I see that it's fortunate that I came for more reasons than just that. You have made a mistake in accepting that man into your pack."

He was pointing at Ash, who looked like he was a heartbeat away from drawing a weapon and trying to gun down our new arrivals.

"You haven't yet introduced yourself to me. You can either do so and ask for permission to be here, or you can leave. I'm not interested in hearing allegations from people who have no regard for tradition."

The flare of power that came off of the leader of the other group was impressive, so much so that some of those around me took a step backwards. An answering surge of energy flashed out from my beast and it was all that I could do to stop a transformation from ripping through me.

"You would be wise to show some respect, Graves. I represent Onyx from the Louisiana pack. If you know what's good for you, you'll hand Hunt over now and avoid the beating you've got coming to you for sheltering him."

I cocked my head at him. Only a complete fool would threaten me like that—a complete fool, or someone who was absolutely confident that he had a bigger stick than I did. I made a note to pump Ash for more information about the New Orleans pack and then I held a hand up and pointed at the nameless leader.

"Leave my territory now and don't return or I'll kill you on sight. Nobody threatens me or my pack with impunity."

"I'll leave, but I'm taking Hunt with me."

He said it as he took a step towards Ash, but I wasn't about to let him take anyone. My beast was in full agreement. On a primal, instinctive level Ash was ours, but more importantly, I wasn't about to let anyone else come in and bleed us the way that Agony had.

I reached for my power. For a split second nothing happened and then it responded in a spectacular manner. All four of the new arrivals dropped bonelessly to the ground between one instant and the next.

I nearly gasped at the sheer amount of power I was pulling from the four of them, but the tiny singularity in my stomach greedily sucked it down and reached for more. I kept my mental fist clenched tight enough to avoid pulling power from anyone else, but it was a battle, much more so than I remembered it being in Chicago.

I absently noticed that this time I could almost feel where the power was being sent after it reached me, but I kept most of my attention on the four crumpled forms on the ground in front of me.

"I warned you. Twice. Neither you, nor anyone else gets to dictate those kinds of terms to me."

I debated between two courses of action for an instant and then turned back to Donovan.

"Donovan, can you please oversee the task of bringing four cages up here? James, Dom and Jess will help you."

I watched as Donovan and the others disappeared into the house and then turned back to the four wolves from Ash's old pack. The leader's gaze was full of hate and I momentarily felt the power coming from him increase as he tried to force himself up onto his feet.

"You won't get away with this. It's only a matter of time until you lose control of your ability and then I'll kill you."

The words were labored but still understandable. It was probably an attempt to get under my skin enough to make me lose my concentration, but if so he failed. I gave him a cold smile as I walked closer to him.

"If you're right then you'd better hope that Donovan returns quickly. If I started to lose control of my power then I'd be forced to just kill you right away."

That shut him up until the first cage arrived. He was the most dangerous so I picked him up and dragged him over to the cage. A second later he was inside and the cage was locked. These cages had been designed with our kind's superior strength in mind, so even the strongest hybrid wouldn't be able to break free once they were locked inside.

James, towering over the rest of us in his hybrid form, dropped the second cage off and then headed back for another one. The two guys we'd caged up started running their mouths as soon as I refocused my ability to exclude them, so I simply dropped them again and ordered Ash to go grab tranquilizers.

I was still amazed at the amount of energy that I was siphoning away from them. It was nearly as much as the entire group of Coun'hij bruisers that I'd incapacitated in Chicago. A few seconds before Jess and Dominic returned with the third cage I felt my absorption field start to wobble.

It had happened before in Chicago, but this time I got a sense that it was wobbling because wherever the power was being sent had started to fill up. I narrowed the focus back down to just the two shape shifters who hadn't been caged and then breathed a sigh of relief when Ash showed back up with a full tranq kit.

"Shut those two idiots up and then inject the two on the ground."

I didn't get to see Ash smile very often, but there was a casual enjoyment to the way that he put darts into all four of the Louisiana wolves. The amount of power coming off of the two who hadn't been caged yet dropped within seconds of their being drugged, but the wobble was back already.

I wanted to just turn off my ability, but instead I played it safe and kept it going until the last of our unwelcome visitors was safely locked up. As I turned back towards the rest of the pack Adri started to collapse. Rachel got an arm around her and lowered her to the ground about the same time that I arrived.

"Are you okay, Adri?"

She looked up at me and nodded. "Yes, sorry. I...I'm feeling a little flushed. I wouldn't have thought that it was enough hotter here to cause me problems."

Rachel was fanning Adri as Donovan came out of the house and headed our way. "I think it's just heat stroke, Alec. If Donovan and I can get her back inside and get some fluids in her she'll be okay."

Adri tried to wave them away. "Alec isn't getting out of dinner with me that easily."

I fought down a smile as I shook my head at her. I'd promised her dinner with just the two of us once everything was settled with her mom. I hadn't expected her mom and Russ to leave so quickly, but she was right, I owed her dinner.

"We can do dinner tomorrow night once you're feeling better, Adri."

She looked up at me with such an expression of disappointment that I relented. "Go with Donovan and Rachel now, and if you're feeling better in an hour or two then we can still do dinner."

I got a nod of acceptance and then watched as the three of them disappeared into the house. Our last three cars were still on their way and it was past time to put a little bit of thought into avoiding another confrontation like we'd just had with Ash's old pack.

James was still standing next to the cages only now he was looking like he wasn't excited about the prospect of carrying them around to the back of the house with an extra few hundred pounds of shape shifter in each of them.

"Where do you want these, Alec? In the garage until we can arrange for a truck?"

"Actually I think maybe it would be best if we just leave them here until after we've greeted the last few visitors. Grab some tarps, please, so we can cover them up until we confirm that our visitors are more of the moonborn, but if they are indeed more of our kind then go ahead and drop the tarps so it's obvious that I'm serious when I give an order."

I motioned for Isaac to help me move the cages around. We positioned them just in front of the arc of the pack and our guests such that it would be easy for the girls to pull the tarps off. My mind wasn't really on the work though. With the eight of us from the pack, assuming you counted Kristin, and the five guests who owed us help if the pack got jumped, we were in pretty good shape. Even if my power only served to keep a group of attackers down for a few seconds it would be enough to allow us to defeat several times our number.

Given that we were relatively safe again, my thoughts instead turned to the dinner that Adri and I would be having either tonight or tomorrow night. I'd planned on making it a special occasion but in light of everything that had just happened I suddenly realized that a change of plans was in order.

This was going to be the most important dinner of my life.

Chapter 3

Adriana Paige
Graves Estate
Sanctuary, Utah

I felt incredibly stupid for having nearly fainted out on the front step while Alec had been dealing with Ash's old pack members. Rachel and Donovan did their best to reassure me that it hadn't been a big deal, but I knew they weren't being completely honest.

Alec needed a pack that could stand at his back without flinching no matter what happened. I'd thought I was prepared for any kind of violence but in the end it had turned out that the heat was too much for me. It had just kind of snuck up on me. One minute I'd been fine and then suddenly I'd just more or less collapsed.

I was resting in the sitting room closest to the kitchen with a protein shake in one hand and a pad and pencil in the other when Alec found me an hour later.

"How are you feeling?"

"I'm okay, sorry for making an idiot out of myself, but okay. I'd really like to have dinner with you still if possible."

Alec put a hand on my forehead and then nodded. "Let's go."

"Now? I need time to get ready."

Given the number that the heat had just done on me, I'd stripped down to one of Jasmin's old tank tops and some capris. Somehow it didn't seem glamorous enough of an outfit to be wearing out on my first date with Alec since we'd broken up.

Alec cocked his head to one side and looked me up and down. "I think you look perfect. Besides, if you put on more clothes than that you'll just overheat again."

He had a point. Also, I didn't really have much else to wear. Rachel had promised, or maybe threatened was a better description, to take me shopping as soon as everything with my mom was squared away. I kept telling her that we should just get my mom to box up my old clothes but she'd refused to cancel the shopping trip because she figured that I might need my New York clothes the next time I happened to be in New York.

Actually, *I* was rich now too, but I honestly didn't understand how Rachel thought sometimes.

Maybe now that my mom had agreed to let me stay I'd be able to convince Alec to take his money back.

Alec gently pulled me to my feet and then led me through the house and out back. He was holding my hand, which was nice, but I was still waiting for the other shoe to drop. Eventually he'd remember that there was a chance he'd addict me to his touch and start cutting down on the physical contact. For now I figured that I'd just soak in being with him and deal with the inevitable freakout when it actually happened.

"Where are you taking me?"

"Dinner, silly."

My face heated up, but I gamely stuck my tongue out at him. "You know what I mean. I half expected that 'a nice dinner' meant that you were going to bundle me into one of the jets and fly to Salt Lake City."

Alec smiled as he shook his head at me. "No, you've pretty much managed to convince me that expensive trips aren't your cup of tea. I thought that maybe a picnic would be more your speed."

"Actually, a picnic sounds perfect."

We walked for several more minutes in companionable silence before coming around a set of hedges and into view of a gorgeous gazebo. The structure was so light and airy that it would have been breathtaking under normal circumstances, but today it was hung with swaths of green silk.

"It's amazing. Just like the Ashure Day Dance."

Alec squeezed my hand and led me up into the gazebo and over to the picnic that he'd had laid out on a blanket. There were green cushions scattered everywhere so that it didn't feel like we were even sitting on the ground.

Once he'd poured me a glass of grape juice and I'd dished up from the seven or eight different dishes that were waiting for us, Alec sighed in contentment.

"It's so nice to be able to leave all of the politics and dominance stuff behind for a little while."

"What happened after I left today?"

Alec popped a grape into his mouth and chewed it to buy himself time, but I wasn't about to let him get away with keeping me in the dark anymore.

"Hey, I'm as deep into this stuff as I'm going to get. The Coun'hij isn't going to let me sit on the sidelines at this point, so I'm better off knowing exactly what is going on."

"You're right, you're right. I guess I'm just a little nervous that I'll say the wrong thing and you'll leave again."

I shook my head. "I'm here for the duration. I know that there are some tough choices ahead, but I want to help you chart a course through them if I can."

Alec nodded and then took a deep breath. "The other three cars were just more envoys from other packs. So now we've also got people here from Flagstaff, Carlsbad and Las Cruces. Pretty much all of the border packs that are within a day or so drive of here with the exception of a couple from California."

"So what do they all want?"

"You saw Raynor and Rebekka. Those two are feeling the situation out, trying to figure out whether or not they can improve their lot by entering into an alliance with us in some form or fashion. Two of the others were the same way, people who are trying to avoid getting crushed between us and the Coun'hij at best, pure opportunists at worst. The last one was different though. The Las Cruces group came to offer an oath of fealty."

My jaw hit the floor. Russ hadn't been far off at all when he'd said Alec was some kind of royalty.

"That's great. The more packs that you can bring to your side the better off we'll be in our efforts to bring down to the Coun'hij."

Alec nodded, but I knew he wasn't convinced, or rather he was worried about something related to our discussion.

"What's wrong?"

He tried to get off with a shrug but I shot him a stern look, which earned me a smile and a real answer.

"With humans it's a lot easier to tell when they are lying. With shape shifters you can still usually catch people in a lie, but not always.

What if one of the people promising to help us is actually just a really good liar? That's a big part of how the monarchy was destroyed the first time around."

I was suddenly incredibly glad that I'd been brainstorming during my hour of forced convalescence. The solution was so obvious that eventually he would have stumbled onto it himself, but this way I got credit for it and he'd maybe start thinking of me as a resource rather than just another person who needed protecting.

"That's easy, Alec. Get Shawn down here to witness their oaths. He'll be able to tell whether or not they intend to keep them and then you'll know exactly who you can and can't trust."

I'd seen Alec less stunned after being hit in the head. It made me want to giggle, but I managed to keep my expression suitably serious.

"You're brilliant, Adri. Shawn won't love the idea, but if we turn it into a big enough bunch of pomp and ceremony then he can just blend into the background and there's a good chance that nobody will know that he's there, let alone the reason he's there. You just solved one of my biggest problems!"

I felt a little flush of pleasure at his tone. This was better by far than his touch. "Okay, hit me with the rest of your problems and let's see if I can solve the rest of them too."

Alec leaned back and gave me a measuring glance. "How about if you tell me what you think my other problems are and what you think I should do about them. I'm interested to see how much you've picked up so far."

Wow, I hadn't expected a test quite so soon. Nothing to do but give it my best shot and hope he was impressed by how much thought I'd put into it at least.

"I think you need to start concentrating your forces. You're a pretty big deterrent all by yourself, but we're going to need more fighters if we're going to really start pushing the Coun'hij. I think you should put out an open invitation to the dispossessed to come in from the cold. Some of them won't be interested and some of them won't be the kind of people you want here, but there are probably at least a few who wouldn't mind being part of a pack again. Given that you're going to be dominant to any of them, you can probably slot them into the power structure inside our pack without anybody getting hurt too badly."

Alec nodded and gave me a check mark in the air. "Very nice. Jasmin must have told you how impressed I was with the way that Jaclyn Annikov has been able to enforce an artificial dominance structure on her pack, but I expect that the idea with the dispossessed was pure Adri."

I nodded and then threw out my only other decent idea. "I think you need to figure out how to unite some packs that are geographically close together. Ulrich agreeing to support you is nice, but he's so far away that we can't do much to help each other. Once you've got a chunk of territory sworn to you then you can shift some of the fighters out of the safer areas into the places where you're most worried about attack by the Coun'hij."

"Well done, Adri. You're exactly right. Do you know what my last problem is?"

I must have looked even more crestfallen than I realized. Alec reached over and lifted my chin up.

"You didn't fail, Adri. I'm impressed. So far, you're ahead of anyone else in the pack other than maybe Ash and Donovan. It's all the more incredible because you didn't grow up thinking in terms like this."

Alec pulled me to my feet and handed me a taper. "Let's get these candles lit. It's going to be dark soon."

As soon as my taper was burning steadily I started moving from candle to candle. It seemed like there were hundreds of them, but it actually only took us about fifteen minutes to finish the process.

The ritual of holding the fire to a wick until the candle started burning was surprisingly calming. I looked over at Alec several times as I was working my way round the edge of the gazebo, and each time he met my gaze I was struck by how content he looked. Alec might not have all of the answers when it came to dealing with the Coun'hij, but he was back to being the confident guy I'd fallen in love with months ago.

Once every candle had a tiny flame slowly dancing above it, Alec and I stepped back to the center of the gazebo and just watched the lights move for several minutes. At some point Alec wrapped his arms around me and I leaned back against him, reveling in the solid feel of his chest behind me.

"Thank you for tonight, Alec. It's perfect. I missed being with you every single day that I was in New York. Being back here is so amazing that sometimes I have to pinch myself to make sure that it isn't all just a dream."

"I missed you too. After you left, everything started falling apart. I tried to hold things together, but it was like I was missing my rudder. Every storm that came through just blew me completely off track. Knowing that you're here, that you still care about me, helps give me hope that we'll be able to weather everything that's coming towards us."

There was something in Alec's voice that told me he was ready to talk about his last major problem. Some girls would have thought that he was ruining a perfectly good moment by taking the conversation back around to his work, but I wasn't one of them. That was just part of who Alec was. He was so incredible exactly because he was willing to take responsibility for so many people. It was one of the things that I loved the most about him.

I turned around so I could look him in the eyes, but left his arms resting on the small of my back. "Out with it. What's the next storm racing towards the pack?"

"Not towards the pack, towards you and me."

"What do you mean?"

"Of the six packs that sent representatives today, four of them are angling for an alliance by way of marriage. That's the only explanation for why they'd have brought so many girls our age with them."

I felt almost like I'd been slapped, but I knew Alec wasn't trying to hurt me, not after preparing such an incredible date. He was trying to equip me with the knowledge I'd need to survive the craziness of watching dozens of incredibly hot shape shifter girls throwing themselves at him.

"So it's Tasha and her mom all over again?"

"Sort of. These girls have the same kind of goal as Tasha had, but I'm not willing to entertain their advances like I was with Tasha. My power finally awakening for real means that I've got options now that I didn't have back then, but more importantly, I know that you still love me. I'm not marrying any of them."

I felt my heartbeat slow back down with the added proof that Alec hadn't brought me here to break up with me. It wouldn't have matched at all with what I knew of his character, but a part of me had still assumed the worst was about to happen.

"Thank you for warning me. I'll try not to get jealous or anything."

Alec's smile was odd, a curious mix of happy and sad. "A warning isn't very much to take into what's coming, Adri. In a shape shifter pack the jockeying for position carries through to more than just who's going to give everyone orders."

The relief that had just washed through me evaporated. "What are you trying to tell me, Alec?"

"When a dominant starts looking for a mate it isn't unusual for the eligible candidates to engage in some pretty spirited competition for the dominant's attention. As things stand right now you'll have half a dozen female shape shifters doing their best to make your life difficult. Even the less aggressive of them will have a hard time believing that I'd really choose a human, not given how much benefit there could be to binding another pack to me via marriage."

My throat had gotten so dry that it was hard to talk. I looked around the gazebo, taking in the silks and the candles as a way of buying myself time. Alec was painting a pretty bleak picture. I'd never dealt very well with the popular girls on the few occasions when I'd roused their ire for some reason or another. What Alec was describing was a hundred times worse than that, but I knew what I had to do, what I wanted to do.

"I'm not leaving, Alec. At least not as long as you still want me. My place is by your side."

He nodded at me, took my hands in his, and then lowered himself down onto one knee. "I didn't want to do it like this. I've known since before Agony came the first time, but in a perfect world I would have given you more time than this."

Alec reached into his pocket and pulled out a velvet box, tiny in his massive hands. "I don't want you to ever think that this was driven by anything other than a pure desire on my part to be with you. If there is any doubt in your mind then refuse me right now and we'll weather the storm the best we can until you're sure."

The box was open now, sparkling with reflected candlelight, but I refused to look directly at it, instead meeting Alec's gaze squarely. Alec took another breath and then smiled, but it wasn't like any of the smiles I'd seen out of him lately. This one was pure happiness and if I'd had any doubt about the sincerity of his proposal that smile would have burned those doubts away.

"Adriana Paige, will you please consent to become my wife?"

Chapter 4

Adriana Paige
Graves Estate
Sanctuary, Utah

The ring was gorgeous, but I didn't even notice until nearly an hour later. I said yes to Alec's proposal, although it might have been fairer to characterize my response as a joyful scream. Alec slid the ring on my finger and pulled me into a kiss while my head was still spinning in astonishment that it had happened.

On the one hand it felt like we'd only known each other for a few days, but on the other hand it seemed like I'd been waiting for Alec to truly claim me for ages. This was an unmistakable sign that I belonged to him and he belonged to me.

I was still giddy with excitement when Alec noticed that the cooling air had me shivering. I wanted to stay out in the gazebo all night but Alec sternly refused my plea.

"You collapsed just a few hours ago. We need to get you inside and keep your body temperature regulated. The last thing that you need right now is to come down with something."

Alec was apparently still just as immune to my pouts as ever. Less than fifteen minutes later all of the candles had been blown out and we were headed back to the house.

Given how little sleep shape shifters needed, it wasn't late enough for everyone else to be in bed, but we didn't run into anyone on our way back which suited me just fine. There would be plenty of time to enjoy being 'officially' engaged. That part could go as long as I wanted it to, but this part would only last for a few more hours or at most a day or two. Right now it was just Alec and I who knew and that was somehow more perfect than anything else I could imagine.

Once we were back in Alec's room with the lights turned down low I finally looked down at the ring and gasped. It wasn't just a ring, it was jewelry perfection. An almost obscenely huge trilliant cut diamond looked up at me from a white setting that I was pretty sure was platinum. The setting cradled the triangular diamond so that none of the sharp corners were exposed but left the large face and most of the edges out where the light could get to them.

There was no questioning the beauty of the ring, but I also got a surprising sense of history as I looked at it. It was shiny and new-looking, but it felt old.

"Alec, where did you get this ring?"

"It was my great-great-grandmother's on my dad's side of the family. There are four or five rings that have been in the family for centuries and out of all of them this is the one that I thought best suited you. Mom has one of the others and Rachel has had a third ring picked since she was seven."

It was too much. I'd been in shock up until now, but the longer I thought about it, the more I became convinced that it was too much. Alec stopped me as I tried to pull it off of my finger.

"Adri, this ring is yours now, unless you're telling me that you don't want to marry me."

"No, I still want to marry you, but I can't wear this. Not only is it an heirloom, it's got to be worth some serious money. What is this diamond, like seven carats?"

Alec shook his head, still holding my hand so that I couldn't pull the diamond off of my finger.

"It's something like four and a half carats, Adri. The setting is platinum and if you disregard the history bit of things, you could buy one like it for less than fifty thousand bucks. It's a really, really nice stone, but on the scale of really excessive jewelry it's only about a six or a seven considering that you'll make many,

many times this each year from your trust fund. Trust me, we've got much more expensive rings in the family, I purposefully chose a more sedate option for you."

Logically I knew he was right. I was ridiculously rich now. The fact that I hadn't earned any of it didn't make the money any less real. It just seemed so crazy. I'd spent weeks despising all of the really rich girls at my school in New York and now I was one of them. I would have said that nothing would have made that worthwhile, but I was realizing that there was one thing that could make me willing to enter into a world that I knew I was profoundly unprepared for.

I debated between a couple of different responses for a few seconds and then looked up and met Alec's gaze. "There's nothing I can do to convince you to buy me a cheaper ring with a normal-sized diamond?"

"I'm sorry, Adri. I know that you're not exactly comfortable with the idea of marrying a billionaire, but honestly this ring is almost too restrained. You need a visible symbol that you're mine. The girls who are going to be coming through here need to be able to see that I value you, that I'm invested in you. Money doesn't prove that, but if you've got a thousand-dollar ring some of them will automatically assume that I'm not taking our engagement seriously. The fact that the ring has been in my family for so long will go a long ways towards offsetting the fact that it's not nearly as expensive as you might otherwise have expected to receive."

Every time I thought I had a handle on what it was really going to mean to be with Alec he threw me for another loop like this. I didn't like his conclusion but I couldn't argue with his logic.

"Okay, I'll wear it, but only on one condition."

"Name it and if I can reasonably do it for you then I will, Adri. You know that."

I took a deep breath and then nodded. "I don't want a long engagement, Alec. If we're going to go through all of the craziness that I suspect is headed full speed towards us, then I want to do it as man and wife."

I didn't realize I'd looked away from Alec again until he tipped my chin back up so that he could see my face.

"Are you sure? That is moving really fast. It means that we've got to get your mom to buy off on the idea, that or we'll have to proceed with getting you emancipated. I'm okay with that, I just don't want you to rush into anything."

I nodded. "I'm sure. A month, two at the outside and then I want us to be married. I don't want to risk something happening before I get a chance to marry you. I'd thought about us before now, but it wasn't until you proposed tonight that I realized that not only is it exactly what I want, there's no reason to wait any longer than I have to."

Alec turned my hand over so that we could both see the ring. "There was more than one reason that I picked this particular ring for you, Adri. The setting shields the points, protecting them, but more importantly stopping them from cutting the wearer or others up. That is what you do for me. You take the most dangerous parts of me and help stop me from doing things that can't be undone."

I started to tear up, but Alec wasn't done. "If you want to get married sooner rather than later then that can happen. It's going to mean a lot of work, but we can hire a wedding planner or two, and Rachel will positively be in heaven at the thought of being able to help you organize everything."

"Wait, you didn't say anything about a big wedding, Alec. I was thinking of a really small ceremony."

Alec's sigh was eloquent and I suddenly realized that he would have preferred a smaller event as well. "I know, but I'm afraid that, given all of the recent changes, we're not going to be able to have what we want in that area. I'm...well, I'm more than just another pack leader. The things I said in Chicago more or less put every wolf in North America on notice that I was choosing to pursue my family's inheritance. I knew it was going to lead to these kinds of problems down the road, but I couldn't come up with any other route that gave me a chance at stopping the Coun'hij."

My knees weren't able to sustain my weight anymore. I dropped down so that I was sitting on the edge of Alec's bed. "So I'm not just marrying Alec Graves, the billionaire, I'm marrying Alec Graves, the future king of the shape shifters."

"I'm afraid so. That means there is a certain level of pomp and ceremony expected for these kinds of occasions. It might be smart to set the wedding date out far enough that you'll have a chance to get used to the idea before the actual day arrives, but I'll do whatever you want. Just understand that once we start down a path there is going to be a lot of inertia. We can't just change our plans at the drop of a hat, not when invitations will be sent out to every pack alpha and half a dozen governors and state senators."

Once again it was hard to get the words out, but even as he'd been painting what was for me a pretty bleak picture, I'd still known what my answer would be. Alec was worth all of that other craziness.

"I understand but I still want to go forward, both with getting married to you, and with the ceremony happening soon."

Alec kissed my forehead and then wrapped his arms around me. "Okay, we'll tell the pack first thing tomorrow and then start the process.

Donovan will probably kick and scream at the impropriety of it all, but we'll make the wedding happen in the next month or two."

"I guess I'd better get busy planning then. A month isn't very long to work with when you're planning the gala event of the year."

Chapter 5

Alec Graves
Graves Estate
Sanctuary, Utah

Adri had spent the night in her own bed, much to her frustration, but I'd insisted. We were still under the threat of sudden death, but we'd made it this far without doing anything inappropriate and I wasn't going to continue to run the risk, especially not if our wedding was less than two months away.

Most of the time Adri seemed to think that my control was unlimited, but it was more finite than I liked to admit. My beast seemed to have decided that Adri was the one for me, and he didn't operate under the same set of rules.

In addition to keeping us both virtuous for the next two months, sleeping in separate beds meant that I could come and go without worrying about waking Adri up. As much as I would have liked to just lie in bed listening to her breathe, I already knew that things were going to get more hectic over the coming months.

It wouldn't be light outside for another hour or two still, but I'd already gotten what sleep I needed, and was now zipping around corners on my R1. I couldn't afford to have someone follow me, so I'd left the motorcycle's headlights off. There was just enough light from the moon for my eyes to see the road. I wouldn't have tried triple digit speeds under these conditions, but I could see well enough that the trip only took an extra ten minutes over what it usually did.

I stabled my bike in the usual place, waited fifteen minutes to make sure that I wasn't being followed, and then made the hike to Mallory's cabin. Mallory must have heard me coming because she answered the door within seconds of my knock.

"Alec, I'm glad you came back. I...I'm sorry for what I said last time you were here."

Three weeks ago I wouldn't have been able to accept her apology, but I'd worked through a lot of things since then. I gave her a gentle hug as I stepped into her tiny cabin.

"It's okay, Mallory. To whatever extent you did anything wrong, I forgive you. I'm sorry too. You weren't entirely wrong, I was just focusing on the wrong pieces of advice. You were right, I needed to man up and deal with the situation, I was just too conflicted at the time to do it."

Mallory gave me a slow, appraising look and then nodded. "You're not conflicted anymore though, are you?"

"No. On the one side I had you and Donovan telling me that I needed to avoid repeating my father's mistakes regardless of the cost, but something inside of me agreed more than I wanted to admit with what Adri had said. I know that you and Donovan have had to deal with all the fallout from my dad's fight with Agony, but I think that he ultimately made the right decision. Maybe he should have made different decisions leading up to the fight, but once he was there and faced with letting Agony kill Donovan I think he made exactly the right decision."

I'd never seen Mallory cry, but her eyes were suspiciously bright now. She nodded her head and then cleared her throat.

"I've had a lot of time on my hands to think about things since we last talked. I...well, I think you've got something there. Kaleb fighting Agony didn't have to be the end of everything. If I hadn't jumped into the fight then Agony would have just killed your father and left. That's all he really wanted, but I couldn't imagine a future without your father."

We shared a few seconds of silence and then she looked back up at me. "What's happened since I saw you last?"

I couldn't help chuckling. Not at her expense, but at the difficulty of encapsulating the last few weeks into a few pithy sentences.

"Things got bad with the dispossessed. The pack pretty much started to implode and we got an offer of alliance from the Tucson pack."

Agony had savaged Mallory's body, but there wasn't anything wrong with her mind. I could already see her trying to fit the new bits of information in with everything else she knew.

"You accepted the offer of alliance and having Jaclyn on our side has solved the problems with the challengers from the dispossessed."

"No, I finally manifested my power in full. We were in Chicago picking up Jasmin and Isaac who'd both been injured in a fight with a werewolf. Agony was there and I fought him to save Jasmin and Isaac. I planned on dying but at the very end of the fight my power came completely awake and I brought everyone in the room to their knees. Before the night was over, I killed Agony and half of the enforcers he brought with him."

If Mallory hadn't already been sitting down she probably would have fallen over. As it was she reached for the arms of her chair with both hands in an effort to steady herself.

"You've done it then. A gift like that, able to operate at distance, makes you nearly unstoppable. The dispossessed will leave you alone and every pack within two hundred miles will be looking for some kind of alliance."

I nodded, happy to see Mallory's expression of relief. "We've already got representatives from five different packs here and four of them are looking for some kind of marriage out of the bargain but last night I proposed to Adri."

"She's back then?"

"Yes, she's back and she accepted. We'll be married in a month or two."

"You're giving up a powerful bargaining chip by marrying her instead of binding one of the other packs more tightly to you."

My beast wanted to take exception to her words but I knew she was just doing what she thought was her duty.

"If the last few months have taught me nothing else, they've taught me that there isn't any halfway on doing the right thing. I was willing to entertain the idea of a political marriage when I thought Adri didn't want me, but not now. Walking away from her and marrying someone I don't love would be wrong on every level. I've realized that being true to myself helps the pack. When I start putting what I perceive as the good of the pack in front of doing what's right then it's a short road to even greater problems."

Mallory knew she was skating up to the very edge, that the Alec that had stormed out of her cabin weeks ago wouldn't take kindly to any more interfering, but in her own way she was just as committed to doing the right thing as I was.

"What about the Ja'tell bond? I'm fond of Adri, but aren't you worried about what the Ja'tell bond will do to her?"

The new me smiled at her concern rather than raging at her. "Adri is stronger than I ever gave her credit for. She hasn't shown any of the signs of addiction and I've come to realize that I should never bet against Adri. She knows what she wants and I'm not going to try and tell her that we shouldn't be together anymore."

Mallory met my eyes for several seconds and then looked down in submission. "I'll advise, Alec, but I won't do any more than that. I've learned my lesson. I knew it years ago when I worked with your father, but I'd forgotten it in the intervening years. You are the one who ultimately has to live with your decisions so they are yours to make."

"Thanks, Mallory. That means a lot, but I hope you're happy for us as well, not just resigned to the fact that we'll get married."

"I am happy for the two of you. I guess I'm just cautious after all of these years. I can't see a happy development without worrying about all of the ways that it could go bad."

I let the silence grow for nearly a minute as Mallory worked through the demons from her past. When she finally leaned back in her chair she'd regained a measure of her calm.

"Alec, can I try to read your power? It's possible that there is something there I can tell you that will help."

"That's part of why I came. I wondered if you'd be able to see it without all of the usual rigmarole now that it is fully active."

Mallory shrugged. "With very powerful or very active abilities I can often see them without coming into contact with the hybrid who has them, but occasionally a power that is more subtle isn't readable without physical contact. Yours sounds like it is something that you have to consciously trigger so it's not necessarily surprising that I haven't been able to get a read on it yet."

I was halfway to her chair when her words hit me. "No, that doesn't sound right. My power is almost always active. It's been doing a kind of low-level drain on everyone around me for weeks. We were half convinced that Rachel was being attacked by some new member of the Coun'hij because she was too tired to get out of bed most days. It's only recently that I've managed to mostly shut it off."

"Are you draining me now?"

"No, but it's taking a real effort. It's like walking around with my hand clenched all of the time. As long as I keep it top of mind I remember to keep the power from pulling at everyone's energy but as soon as I stop thinking about it my mental 'fist' relaxes and I start draining people a little again."

Mallory was intrigued now. Before she'd been exiled to this cabin she'd made a study of every living hybrid she'd been able to get her hands on. In a very real sense she was the world's best expert on the abilities manifested by a small subset of the hybrids among our people.

"That *is* interesting. Come here and let me take a look at you and then we'll go from there."

I knelt in front of her chair and then waited as she placed a hand on either side of my face. As the minutes passed perspiration started to bead Mallory's forehead, and her grip tightened, but I didn't interrupt her. When she finally let go of me and slumped back into her chair it was obvious that she wasn't satisfied with the results of her scan.

"What did you see?"

"Nothing. No, not quite nothing, but not what I'd hoped. Your power is active, you've got the same increase in your overall energy level that I usually see when a hybrid finally manifests a power, but I can't get in close enough to get a good look at what you do. My mental probes keep disintegrating as soon as I send them in. I tried making them more powerful, but I still got only impressions of things rather than anything solid."

"I'll take impressions at this point. I know next to nothing so even an impression is a step up."

Mallory seemed to debate for a couple of seconds and then she shook her head. "Go ahead and activate your power on me first and then we'll talk. Start small and then you can work up."

I nodded and then relaxed my grip on my power. Only a trickle at first, but then wider and wider until Mallory started a boneless slide out of her chair. I caught her and then shut my ability back down as I helped her back into her chair.

Mallory sat there for several seconds, considering what had just happened. "Interesting. What else can you tell me? You've used it several times by now, have *you* gotten any impressions as you've done so?"

I shrugged. "Not much definitive. I can target where I draw from rather than just dropping everyone around me, but sometimes if I try and take in too much at once it sort of wobbles. I got the feeling last time that the power I'm pulling from everyone is going somewhere and that there was only so much power that I could pull in before that reservoir would fill up."

Mallory started absently tapping the arm of her chair. "That is potentially problematic. If it's true it would mean that you'd want to husband the use of your power to make sure that you always had the ability to absorb however much power you needed to."

"I know, I had the same thought, but I don't love the implication. Will the reservoir gradually empty back out or have I already pretty much shot my bolt?"

Mallory's smile and shrug were sympathetic, but she obviously didn't know any more at this point than I did.

"I would tend to doubt that to be the case, Alec. Our abilities are still governed by natural rules and laws, they just sometimes exploit them in ways that modern science still can't explain. My suspicion would be that the power you're sending will tend to dissipate out of whatever container it is housed in. Things tend to move from high concentration to low concentration, so the simple passage of time should help empty your 'reservoir' out."

I breathed a sigh of relief. It wasn't a guarantee, but at least it offered some hope that I'd still be able to protect my friends and family.

Mallory looked like she wanted to get up and pace, but she forced her hands still and then looked back up at me. "I can offer only two other pieces of advice. Until you know more, don't use your power cavalierly, but at the same time don't hoard your power when you are in danger. The ability to drop four people at once does you no good if you let one person kill you because you were trying to protect yourself against that future four-person threat."

"That makes sense. I need to bind some of the other packs to me sooner rather than later so that I've got resources to stave off minor threats or I could find myself always depleting my ability in order to deal with penny-ante stuff. What was the other bit of counsel?"

She was debating on what to tell me again. She was trying to keep her uncertainty off of her face, but I'd spent too much time with her and she'd spent too much time by herself for her to fool me.

"Keep an open mind about your power. With active powers like the one you have, it is possible sometimes that it isn't the power that comes up short, it's your own belief in what the power can do that stops you from achieving what you otherwise might."

I'd never heard anything like that before, at least not in so many words. It did, however, make me think of the one time I'd met Tasha's mother.

"Jaclyn Annikov once said that she believed her power was triggered by need, that it didn't appear until she had something really important on the line."

Mallory's smile was sad. "That's fitting. Jaclyn is an example of someone who limited herself. The last time I saw her she was using her ability at much less than half of her potential but she was so convinced that she was operating at the very edges of her capability that there wasn't anything I could do to convince her otherwise."

I swallowed a couple of times while I processed what Mallory had just said. "She's already incredibly powerful."

"Yes, she is. I suspect that she's hitting with a larger charge now than she was twenty years ago, but she has the potential to strike with power much more akin to a lightning strike than a Taser. She could quite literally kill with a touch if she just believed herself capable of doing so."

It was a sobering picture. Not just the idea of Jaclyn killing other hybrids with a discharge several times what she was currently capable of, but the thought that she'd limited herself in such an arbitrary fashion. How many times over the years had she lost a pack member because she hadn't been able to recruit the full measure of her ability? If she'd hit Anton with that kind of power he might not have shrugged it off quite so easily. Ash and Kristin would never have met and Jaclyn's pack wouldn't have lost all of the wolves that Anton had killed. I pulled my focus back to the present and speared Mallory with my gaze.

"What aren't you telling me, Mallory? I'm better off knowing it rather than guessing."

Mallory sighed and put her hands up in surrender. "It's more of the same. I can't see the specifics of your ability, but you glow more powerfully than anyone else I've ever seen, even your father."

I shrugged. "Dad made good use of his ability, but it was hardly game-changing."

Mallory shook her head. "Your father's death was one of the greatest tragedies since the fall of the monarchy. His primary power was his ability to heal, but he actually had a secondary power."

"I didn't even know that was possible!"

"Neither did I until I scanned him myself. He didn't even develop it until a couple of years before you were born."

"What was it?"

"Your father's healing ability came from a natural affinity to life. He had the ability to bring a similar kind of affinity out in others."

She was dancing around the answer, but it was the missing piece of something that I'd never been able to explain.

"The population explosion in the pack. He caused it, didn't he?"

"Yes, yes, he did. It was statistically impossible and I suspect it was part of what brought things to a head with the Coun'hij. Nearly every mated pair in the pack had a child within a few months of each other despite the fact that most of our kind will try for years before actually having a child."

It was almost too amazing for words. No wonder Mallory had been struggling to just come right out and say it.

"If he'd had another fifteen years the pack would have been unstoppable. Who else knew?"

"Just me. We tried to keep the births quiet, tried to dismiss them as nothing more than an odd fluke, but the Coun'hij could read the writing on the wall as well as you just did. The pack would have increased by fifteen or sixteen moonborn within the next decade and a half, which would have been a significant increase to our combat power, and there would probably have been another crop of children born within the next three to five years."

I wanted to yell or throw things, but nothing I could do now could change the past. We were a tiny race that, even in the best of times, grew incredibly slowly. Every time we had a solid push from south of the border we risked being destroyed as a species. Dad had represented a chance to change all of that. He could have triggered a population boom that would have finally put us in a position to bring order to South America, or to end the vampire scourge that was bleeding the East Coast practically dry. When Agony had killed my father he truly had robbed our people of a great treasure.

"I...I guess I understand why you haven't told me any of that before, but why now?"

"Like I said, Alec. You're more powerful than your father. It's possible that something about the way your gift works requires much more power to produce even a slight impact to the world around you, but I'm not convinced that your gift has revealed everything that it can do. It would be hard to really explain just how much power went into increasing the fertility of the pack back in your father's day."

I took a deep breath and then pushed all of the things that Mallory had just told me to one side. "I'll need to think about all of that some more later, but that's not the only reason that I came by this morning. I'd like to invite you to come live at the house with us again."

Mallory couldn't have been more floored if I'd knocked her into a wall. She considered my invitation and then pulled her legs up onto her chair so that she was huddled into a ball. "Have you mentioned this to Donovan?"

"Not yet, but he's no idiot. Once he really gets his mind around the fact that we've pissed the Coun'hij off as much as we're going to, it logically follows that there isn't any reason to keep you hidden anymore."

"You're right, but he may suffer from some of the same blind spots as me. I'm not sure I would have ever thought of leaving here. It's been my home for so long now that I'd stopped even imagining a day when I might be free to come and go as I please."

"Well, now that I've brought it up, what do you think?"

"I'd like to, Alec, I really would. It might be best though to leave me as a hidden asset for now. You can always bring me out at a later point, but once it becomes general knowledge that I'm still alive, that isn't something that we can take back."

I pursed my lips and nodded, but I wasn't convinced. "You're right that this isn't a step we can undo, but you'd be a much greater asset back at the estate than you are here. Your analysis of events will be much better if you're witnessing them firsthand."

"I know I seem like a scared old woman, Alec, but I need some time to think it over. It's a big change. My head says that you're right, that I may as well be there with you and Donovan, but my heart isn't so sure. The last time my world changed in such a fundamental way was when Agony came through town the first time. Can I have a few days before you mention the possibility to Donovan?"

"Of course you can have some time. I'm anxious to bring you in out of the cold though. We've got a lot more moonborn running around the mansion these days now than we used to. If we leave you here long enough someone is going to get adventurous and stumble onto this place."

Chapter 6

Adriana Paige
Graves Estate
Sanctuary, Utah

"What do you think, Adri? I think this shade of blue would be perfect."

Rachel was a wedding planning machine. We'd spent the morning trying about fifty different cake samples and then she'd jumped right into colors. I appreciated her help, I just hadn't realized things were going to get quite this crazy. Every time I felt like I had a handle on everything that was going to be involved, Rachel came up with another set of decisions that hadn't even crossed my mind.

It was like being washed away in a tsunami of flowers and fabric swatches. Rachel was dead set on me needing a big-name designer for my dress, but I didn't even recognize any of the names she was throwing around. Rach was more than happy to pull together pictures, lots and lots of pictures, of each of their work, but I suspected that deciding on a designer was still going to take up most of tomorrow.

I wanted to marry Alec more than anything, but more and more I wished that we could just be two normal people who didn't have to worry about anything more than keeping our families from fighting with each other at the practice dinner.

I was looking for an excuse to take a break from all of the wedding planning when Ash stuck his head in Rachel's room.

"Can I disturb the two of you for a few minutes?"

Rach bounced up off of her bed and spun through a pirouette with multicolored swatches of fabric in each hand.

"Sure, Ash. What do you need?"

It was amazing how much different Rachel was now from the exhausted, barely functioning girl that Dom had described to me while I'd been in New York. If anything Rachel was actually more energetic and exuberant than I remembered her being from before. It was like she was making up for lost time. Ash shook his head, not in disapproval necessarily, more like he was just as astonished as I was at Rachel's excitement.

"Actually, Alec asked me to steal Adri for a couple of hours."

Rachel sighed, but perked up again only a moment later. "That's okay. I need to catch up on some homework anyways. Alec agreeing to homeschool me for two months while we prep for the wedding was a stroke of genius, but I still have to spend some time doing homework. Besides, this will give me a chance to start pulling together some of those portfolios we talked about."

I followed Ash down the hall in silence. I still didn't know Ash very well. He'd joined the pack while I'd been away so I didn't have the same kind of bond with him that I had with the others. Alec seemed to trust him completely though, so I figured that he was both dependable and incredibly deadly with the weapons he routinely wore.

"Did Alec say what he wanted, Ash?"

"Not exactly. I get the feeling that I'm not supposed to know what's going on. Alec implied a bunch of things but didn't confirm anything."

"Does that bother you?"

"A little, but not as much as you might think. Not as much as I expected it to. I didn't press him on it at least, so it must not be too big of a problem for me. I guess I trust that Alec is smart enough not to keep anything from me that I'll need to do my job. Beyond that, I understand the concept of need-to-know."

I chewed on that for several seconds as Ash led me through the house. He slowed momentarily as we turned a corner. "Truth be told, Adri, there's only one thing that is bothering me and that is the way that Alec is refusing to be pinned down on when he's going to help me resolve things with my old pack."

It took me a second to fit all of the memories together. "Weren't those the ones Alec put in cages on the day that...well, the day that he proposed to me?"

Ash nodded. "Yeah, those four were from my old pack, but I need help if I'm going to go in and get my sister out from under Onyx's thumb. Just mention to Alec that we talked about it when you have a few minutes."

"Okay, I can do that. I don't know that it will do any good, but I can let him know."

Ash gave me a tired smile. "You're going to get a lot more of that now that you are engaged to Alec. It's proof that he trusts you and values your opinion. More and more of the shape shifters that we've got arriving every day are going to try and use you as a way to get Alec's ear."

It had never even crossed my mind, but it made sense. "Thanks for the warning, Ash. I'll definitely keep my guard up, after I help you out of course."

The grin I got this time was surprisingly boyish and unrestrained. I could see why Kristin found him so irresistible.

Ash came to a stop and pointed at a door. "This is it. I dropped off a certain VIP here a few minutes ago. They'll be waiting for you inside."

I nodded and opened the door as Ash turned and walked away. This wasn't a part of the house that I'd been to before, so I had no idea what to expect, but I still somehow ended up being taken off guard when I found myself inside a tiny little room with no windows. The only other features were a heavy door on the far wall and a video camera and a speaker up close to the ceiling.

I tried the far door, but it was locked. I was about to turn around and leave when the speaker hummed to life.

"Try the door again, Adri. I think I found the release button."

I'd been starting to get worried until I heard the voice, which was unmistakably Shawn's. A few seconds later I was inside a slightly larger room that had several monitors and a pair of chairs. Shawn looked up at me from one of the chairs as he waved me over to the other one.

"I hear that this little exercise was your idea. It's the logical solution to your problem, but it means that I'm going to be commuting from Chicago every couple of days so I thought it only fair that you be the one to help me out."

"With what?"

Shawn gestured at the monitors and then pushed a button and the tiny room was full of noise. It took me a second to realize that the monitors were showing Alec and a slew of other people from several different angles and the 'noise' was the audio from the room.

"We get to watch the first royal court in centuries. Alec is going to parade everyone who's come to town so far through that room, which incidentally is only a dozen or so feet away from this room. Each of your guests will then either provide Alec with an oath of fealty or at the very least a promise that they'll behave and live up to the traditional duties of a guest. You and I get to watch it all so that I can tell Alec which ones are really planning on living up to their oaths."

"Why me?"

"Nobody is supposed to know that I'm here. Ash knows now, but even he doesn't know about my power. You're here because I need a pretext for being here that doesn't involve being the world's first living lie detector. Alec gave Ash the impression that I'm educating you on the various shape shifters who will be coming through the room over the next couple of hours."

I nodded. It was kind of a threadbare pretext, but Ash didn't seem inclined to pick at it so it should be enough. Shawn waited to see if I had any questions and then handed me a radio.

"Ash is wearing an earpiece so if we have any questions you can ask him, just push that button and you're live. Everyone is going to be announced though so hopefully we won't have to bug him too much."

Shawn and I quickly settled into a division of duties. He did a screen capture of each of the shape shifters who came before Alec and printed it out while the small talk occurred. I wrote the name of the shape shifters at the bottom of the picture and then flipped the page over and took notes on Shawn's impression of our visitors.

Alec seemed to generally be working from least trustworthy to more dependable. The first few were uneventful but disgusting. The pack leaders practically tied themselves in knots trying to avoid giving Alec a straight answer while their daughters all but threw themselves at Alec.

I could tell that Alec was starting to lose patience by the time the fifth delegation was led away. He kept having to pointedly remind the girls that he was engaged to me and even without Shawn's power it would have been apparent that none of these alphas were planning on throwing their lot in with Alec unless they thought they could come out on top in the negotiations.

A capable-looking woman named Rebekka was the first real surprise. She entered the room looking resigned, but not necessarily unhappy. Alec, Ash at his shoulder, watched her approach to within five feet of him and then welcomed her and thanked her for making time in her schedule for a formal reception.

The room was large enough to hold everyone who had come before and most of them had stayed after being presented to Alec. I saw boredom on more than one face right up until Rebekka dropped to one knee.

"It's not in me to play games, Alec. The Tonopah pack has fallen on rough times and everyone here knows it. I came here hoping that my Vivian would catch your eye, but I'm not going to try and come between two people who love each other, not when there are other options. If you'll have me, I'll swear fealty to you. Your father was an honorable man and you seem to be cut from the same cloth."

Alec took a deep breath and nodded. "I welcome you into my service, Rebekka. You may proceed."

"I swear my claws and fangs to your service, both those of this body and those sworn to me. In return for your protection I will obey your command and never betray your trust as long as you're true to your oath."

Alec stood and walked forward so that he could place a hand on Rebekka's shoulder. "I accept your oath and place myself as a shield between your pack and those who would harm it. I promise justice tempered with mercy and for as long as you are true to your oath I promise to treat you as one of my pack with all of the rights and privileges of family."

Alec pulled Rebekka to her feet and pointed at a spot behind the chair where he'd been sitting. "I understand if you have other business to attend to, but if you're planning on staying for the rest of the reception you're welcome to stand with Ash at my back."

Even I could see that Alec was making a powerful statement with that invitation. Those who had refused to swear fealty to him were exiled to the edges of the room while those who bound themselves to him would stand close enough to advise him.

Shawn shook himself and took a deep breath, almost like he hadn't breathed for several seconds while the oath had been said.

"Complete conviction on both sides. Alec meant every word, as did Rebekka. This was the break that Alec was looking for."

I wrote Shawn's words down verbatim on the back of the paper and then looked up in time to catch the very end of what Alec was telling Rebekka.

"...appreciate the gesture, but Vivian is welcome here."

Rebekka nodded as she took her place just behind Alec, and then the next few delegations were introduced. The alphas who followed Rebekka weren't any more willing to be pinned down than the first few had been, but there was a subtle change to the mood of those who were watching and that made each new arrival more cautious than the one before. The girls they'd brought to try and catch Alec's eye were less and less forward as time went on.

If we'd struck pay dirt with Rebekka, we doubled down with the Las Cruces pack. Their leader swore fealty to Alec with even less hesitation than Rebekka had. Shawn confirmed that the oath had been binding on both sides as the Las Cruces alpha took up a position behind Alec.

The last few arrivals all seemed to be from the dispossessed, which surprised me, but which Shawn didn't seem to think was out of the ordinary. What did surprise me was that the first two, scared-looking wolves who obviously weren't the least bit dominant, lied when they swore fealty to Alec.

I watched as they both took position behind Alec and felt my stomach clench at the thought of them being within striking distance of him.

"What is he going to do with them once he knows that they can't be trusted?"

Shawn shrugged. "I'm not sure. His best bet would be to keep them busy with some task that's important but which they can't use to cause problems. Maybe hunting down werewolves. He might try using them to hold the border or to go after groups of vampires, but there's more risk there because they might tip off their prey and get other wolves killed."

Shawn's lack of concern settled me down a little, but I was starting to realize just how deep the waters Alec was swimming in really were.

Two more dispossessed came through one at a time to swear fealty and Shawn confirmed that they both meant it, although one of them was going to struggle to deliver on his promise.

"He's got too much of a temper, that or just has too hard of a time controlling his beast. Either way he's going to be trouble at some point. Alec's best bet would be to get his beast to swear fealty too in a binding ritual of power."

"Can Alec do that?

"Alec can do it if anyone can. If this guy's original alpha could have gotten his beast to swear allegiance then he probably would have been a valuable member of the pack, but as it was he caused more problems than he was worth."

"Is that why most wolves end up dispossessed?"

Shawn tapped the desk in front of us for a couple of seconds before shaking his head. "There isn't really a 'normal' reason why someone ends up out on their own. Sometimes they are a submissive who just takes too much crap from their original pack so they figure out how to get away and just disappear. Sometimes they grow up never knowing their shape shifter parent so they don't start out in a pack. Sometimes they are too much trouble for their alpha to put up with. Sometimes they have the stuff to take over the pack but know that doing so would make the pack worse off so they leave."

I let his explanation sink in for a minute and then cleared my throat. "But it's not something a wolf would choose lightly, right?"

"Not generally, no. You come across the occasional antisocial moonborn, but for the most part we prefer the company of a pack to being alone. Just as important though is the fact that we all know just how dangerous it is out there. A pack provides a measure of protection from the vampires, werewolves, and other assorted creepy-crawlies."

Whatever else Shawn was planning on saying next went by the wayside as the next set of visitors entered the room. Shawn sat up in his chair and zoomed in on the three newcomers. The printer started humming as he absently sent the screenshot to it, but it was obvious that he was focused on the leader.

"Shawn, who is that?"

"His name is Grayson. He keeps a pretty low profile, but he's one of the dispossessed, at least I thought he was."

"What do you mean you *thought* he was?"

"He's got a rather unique power. Dad made him an offer to try and bring him into our pack as an asset, but Grayson said no. He turned down an absolutely obscene amount of money without batting an eye. Dad was pissed, but there wasn't anything he could do about it."

I started to ask another question, but Shawn was fiddling with the volume on the audio feed so I shut up and just listened instead as Ash announced the newest arrivals.

"Grayson, Wyatt, and Carson."

Just from the expression on Shawn's face I could tell that it wasn't normal for three of the dispossessed to show up at one time like this. Alec and Ash's expressions didn't give that kind of information away, but a wave of trepidation washed through me as I realized that Shawn hadn't actually told me what Grayson's power was.

"Greetings. May I ask why the three of you are here in my territory unannounced?"

Grayson's face didn't give any more away than Alec's, but one of the two guys behind Grayson didn't look happy to be there.

"My brothers and I are here to offer our service to your house."

Alec nodded. "I've accepted oaths of fealty from a number of individuals today, I would welcome yours as well."

Grayson shook his head and I suddenly realized just how big he was. He towered over Ash and the other people behind Alec. "You misunderstand me. Our oaths are not ours to give, but we would serve with your people for a time before returning to other responsibilities."

Outwardly Alec gave no sign of it, but I knew he was running different mental scenarios as he tried to come up with the best possible response to this development.

"Your offer poses some difficulties for me. I'll not expose my people to more danger by welcoming you into our territory and making you privy to my plans and then have you depart abruptly, possibly taking everything you've learned to my enemies."

Grayson nodded his head fractionally. "I believe a compromise can be reached. We could promise to obey all of your commands for a set period of time and agree that we wouldn't reveal anything that could harm your operations, both during the period of service and after."

Alec cocked his head slightly to the side. "Why would you possibly be interested in that kind of oath?"

"Our reasons are our own, it only remains to be seen whether or not you'll accept our oath."

Alec considered Grayson and the others for several seconds before nodding. "Very well, I'll accept your oaths for a minimum of two months and in return promise not to expose you to any risk that I wouldn't accept myself or set you to any task which *I* wouldn't be willing to do."

Grayson bowed his head. "That would be acceptable, but there is one last thing before I can agree." Between one second and the next, Grayson's hybrid form ripped through his clothes and sprang towards Alec.

I opened my mouth to scream and then felt it snap back shut as a wave of convulsions tore through my body. As my head flopped to one side I saw that Shawn's muscles had locked up too.

My head whipped back around in an involuntary motion just in time for me to see Grayson crash into Alec, but Alec didn't even bother changing forms. Out of everyone in the room, he was the only one who wasn't fighting off convulsions.

I was sure that it was Grayson who had caused everyone's bodies to stop working, but it seemed to be causing him problems as well. His twitches weren't as severe as everyone else's but he was still struggling as he tried to bring his claws around to slash at Alec.

Alec calmly stepped back away from Grayson and then suddenly the convulsions left me. As I scanned the monitor I realized that everyone behind Alec was now back to normal, but Grayson and everyone else in the room were still flailing about. Grayson gathered himself for another attack, but Alec gestured and Grayson went down like his strings had been cut. As soon as Grayson hit the floor everyone else's convulsions disappeared.

"I could kill you right now. Are you satisfied with my prowess?"

Grayson managed a tiny nod despite the draining effect of Alec's ability, and then Alec turned it off. I looked away, my face heating up, as Grayson changed back to human shape, but

Shawn's gasp brought me back around. He'd frozen the largest monitor and zoomed in on Grayson's chest.

The bulging muscles looked exactly like I expected them to with one exception. There was a ridge of raised skin in a perfect circle over his heart, forming a white 'O' across otherwise unmarred flesh.

I would have asked Shawn what it meant, but Kristin chose that instant to hurry into the reception hall. The meaning of Grayson's scar was going to have to wait. I didn't know Kristin very well still, but she was a tough cookie. There was only one thing that would make her interrupt Alec like that. She'd just had a dream and it wasn't good news.

Chapter 7

Alec Graves
Graves Estate
Sanctuary, Utah

Kristin rubbed her temples and sighed. "I don't know, Alec. I just can't explain it."

I held a hand up, trying to calm her down. "It's okay, Kristin, nobody is angry at you, I'm just trying to understand what's going on."

Ash looked like he wanted to intervene but I stopped him with a look. I'd kept this discussion just between him, Kristin, Donovan, Louis, Rebekka, and me but it hadn't been easy. Kristin had been understandably rattled by her dream, but rushing into the reception and all but announcing that the Coun'hij was about to attack us hadn't been very prudent.

Donovan cleared his throat, obviously uneasy in the presence of the alphas from Tonopah and

Las Cruces. "Maybe if you were to just run through what you remember again, someone will think of something."

Kristin took a deep breath and nodded. "I fell asleep while I was studying for my GED and I started dreaming about Sanctuary. It was like I was floating a hundred feet above the ground and then suddenly dozens of werewolves were running towards the estate."

Louis' voice came out as a deep rumble. "Which direction were they attacking from?"

"The south."

"You're sure?"

The follow-up question didn't seem to bother Kristin. "Yes. I remember thinking that I needed to orient myself. I looked for the biggest set of mountains and the werewolves were definitely coming at us from the south. Once I found the mountain range I even found that old highway that runs up from Arizona."

Ash and I both leaned forward slightly. This was new. Kristin hadn't ever been wrong before, at least not when it came to the big picture, so when she'd told us that she'd seen an attack coming we'd just started working through contingency plans and put our visitors on high alert.

Those who had just been here as guests rather than allies had mostly departed and then we'd all spent a tense three days expecting an attack at any point. The attack still hadn't materialized, which had some of my allies more jittery about my actions over the last few hours than they otherwise would have been.

Ash looked at me as if to let me ask the question, but I nodded for him to go ahead. Kristin always responded better to Ash than to anyone else.

"Were there vehicles on the road?"

Kristin nodded, but now something new was bothering her. "There were a few cars, a SUV and some kind of cargo truck, but nobody freaked out so they must not have seen the werewolves."

There was a pause and then Kristin shrugged, almost like she was putting whatever had been bothering her out of her mind, and then she continued. "Once the attackers arrived at the estate I only caught flashes of things. I saw Alec pulled down by a pair of them out in the garden and then everyone scattered. You put a bunch of rounds into one from the roof, Ash, but then it jumped up there with you and practically tore you in half."

Reliving the memory was obviously hard on Kristin, but she managed to continue with only a slight catch to her voice. "James and Isaac tried to double-team one of the werewolves out by the garage, like they were trying to buy time for some kind of getaway, but they didn't last long either."

It was my turn to ask the questions. "Did you see any of them inside the house, Kristin?"

"No, I was still just kind of floating above everything while the fight was going on."

"Did you see anyone else? Louis, Rebekka, Jasmin, Dominic?"

"No, just you, Ash, James and Isaac."

Donovan seemed to have figured out where I was headed. He was fumbling through a stack of papers on his desk.

"Here it is. Demolition on the Adams Bridge was started the day *before* Kristin had her dream."

I nodded. "That's what I thought I remembered from our discussion two weeks ago. You'll need to confirm when they had it torn down enough that it wasn't drivable, but I'd be very surprised if it was still navigable by the time Kristin fell asleep."

Kristin was a quick study, but there was just too much she hadn't had a chance to learn yet. "What are you saying, Alec? That my gift isn't working anymore?"

"No, I'm saying that I don't think this was a precognitive dream, I think it was implanted inside your mind by an outside force."

Rebekka and Louis were both nodding now, but it was Ash who gave Kristin the last piece. "Dream Stealer. It all makes sense when you factor him into the picture. Your point of view wasn't from the ground, which is what you're most familiar with, it was from above which he could experience for himself with a simple flyover."

Kristin understood now. "Right, and I saw the four of you die because you are the four who in his mind are key to protecting the pack. I didn't see anyone else because Dream Stealer wouldn't have known that we're allied with Tonopah and Las Cruces."

I waited while everyone settled back down and then started ticking off the key points. "This means that we'll have to take all of Kristin's precognitive warnings with a grain of salt. Even if the Coun'hij isn't ready to attack us, they'll do this kind of thing as a way of keeping us off balance and paralyzed, so we're going to have to be very careful about letting another such attempt delay us from doing stuff that we know is important."

Rebekka nodded. "You're right. In hindsight, you were right to send that group out earlier today, even if you haven't been willing to tell us what it was for yet."

I checked the clock on the wall and then sighed as I reached for the door. "Actually, they are past due to be back. I'd better make a call."

The sound of angry footsteps out in the hall was unmistakable, but if any of us had been too slow to figure that out, Jaclyn's tone would have easily made the point.

"Don't bother with a call, Alec. Instead tell me why you thought you could get away with sending eight of your people down into my area unannounced with an invitation to come here that was little more than a veiled threat."

I pulled the door the rest of the way open and motioned Jaclyn and Tasha inside. James gave me a questioning look from a few feet behind them, but I waved him off. Donovan's office was already filled to capacity. We were going to need to go about getting a larger room ready for these kinds of councils. I made a mental note to ask Donovan what room my father had used and then turned back to Jaclyn.

"The group I sent down was under instructions to extend an invitation, nothing more than that. I would have called ahead, but Tasha isn't exactly taking my phone calls these days. As to the size of the group, it didn't seem fair to bring you up here and leave your pack uncovered. I thought you'd appreciate the four who remained down there to help protect your territory."

There was a challenging look in her eye. "And the four who escorted me back here?"

"Believe it or not, they were for your protection. You don't have anything to worry about from a normal opponent, but given the state of things right now, it's entirely possible that we'll see a rash of werewolves come through this little corner of the state before all is said and done."

Jaclyn seemed a little mollified. She dropped down into the chair next to Tasha, who'd so far refused to meet my gaze. "Fine, your actions weren't quite as unreasonable as I initially thought, but I'm not one of your lackeys to just jump on a plane whenever you call."

I sighed. Things were moving too quickly and I didn't have enough manpower to jump through all of the hoops that tradition stipulated. I'd hoped that our past history together, tenuous though it was, would stop Jaclyn from being quite so offended.

"I truly am sorry for being so high-handed, Jaclyn. I would have just flown down to see you, but my hands are tied right now. I owe guest protection to a number of people and while I can't magically stop a horde of werewolves from decimating the estate, there is a very real possibility that my presence is the only thing keeping the Coun'hij from sending in twenty or thirty enforcers to level everything in the area."

Jaclyn steepled her fingers and then looked at me over the top of them. "Okay, you're sorry and I'll overlook the offense this time. What do you want?"

"Two things. Firstly I want to complete the joining we discussed last month."

"I'm not sure Tasha will take you at this point, Alec. Besides, I've heard talk of an engagement to some human."

Jaclyn was trying to rile me up, but she wasn't going to succeed. I held all of the cards right now and we both knew it.

"While I have the highest respect for Tasha, you're right that a wedding is out of the question, but that's no longer a prerequisite for the kind of alliance that I'm after. Frankly, I'm not overly concerned with the form of the alliance. Within certain limits I'm game for just about anything you're interested in proposing, but I need the Tucson pack and you in particular."

Jaclyn shook her head. "You absolutely care what form the alliance takes. This is nothing like we discussed unless you're really offering to come down off of the little throne you're building yourself and join the Tucson pack."

My beast took exception to that comment, but I forced the surge of power down to something barely more than a flicker and offered Jaclyn a cold smile.

"This is exactly what we were discussing previously. The weaker pack will join the stronger pack in return for a greater degree of protection."

Jaclyn surged to her feet with a flare of power and I reached for my ability, but she hadn't changed shapes yet so I didn't take the chains off of my pocket nuke.

"You've yet to prove that you're more powerful than me, Alec. You go too far in making that kind of statement. You killed Agony. So what? I could have done that years ago."

I turned to those who had been in the room before Jaclyn and Tasha arrived and asked them to leave. Ash tried to protest but I shut him up with a look. Jaclyn was an impatient buzzsaw of power off to my left as everyone filed out of the office. Once it was just Jaclyn, Tasha and I, I turned back to the two women.

"A wise woman once told me that it was smart to settle the issue of dominance right up front. I take no joy in this."

Jaclyn sprang at me as the words left my mouth, but I'd already opened my mental fist nearly as far as it would go. She transformed mid-leap, but I stepped to the side and plucked her out of the air, gently bringing her to the ground so that she wouldn't be injured.

Tasha had slid out of her chair and looked up at me with anger in her eyes but a complete inability to move. I looked back at Jaclyn and sighed.

"You could still kill me if you caught me by surprise, but there can't be any question between you and me as to who is dominant to whom. All of the reasons that caused you originally to consider an alliance with me are still in operation. I'm just bringing infinitely more to the table now than I was back then."

Jaclyn wasn't happy. She pushed against my ability, momentarily flooding it with enough power that she was nearly able to sit back up, but I just opened the channel up even wider. It was enough to cause her to slump back down, but she hadn't given in yet, I could see it in her eyes.

I did the only other thing I could. I grabbed the oversized sweater off of the back of Donovan's chair, draped it across Jaclyn's torso for modesty's sake, and then took the last bit of restraint off of the hungry hole in my abdomen.

The absorption wobbled momentarily as the void on the other end nearly reached its capacity, and then it happened. Jaclyn shrank back down to the smaller shape she'd worn when she'd walked into the room, only it wasn't her choice. She'd wanted to remain a hybrid and continue to fight me but I'd temporarily robbed her of the energy she needed to manifest any other form but the one she'd been born with.

For the briefest of moments Jaclyn stopped breathing and then I closed off my ability and stepped back so that she could pull herself into a sitting position.

"I didn't know that was possible."

"It wasn't, not until a little while ago when my ability finally manifested fully."

The shock was starting to wear off. Jaclyn was scared, but she was also as dominant as anyone else alive.

"So this is it? You'll just kidnap the other alphas and beat them into submission one at a time until you've replaced the Coun'hij as our evil overlords?"

This time my beast wouldn't be denied. I managed to hold onto my shape by the thinnest of margins, but I couldn't stop the arc of energy that rushed out from me.

"I'm not going to force anyone to swear fealty to me, Jaclyn, but you needed to know just exactly what I'm capable of now. I want your help, but if you refuse me then I'll put you back on a plane and that will be that."

I could tell by the look in her eyes that she was finally listening to me.

"You said that you brought us here for two reasons. What was the other thing you wanted?"

"Agony is dead and the Coun'hij has been knocked back on their heels for the first time in centuries. I want you to open up the southern border."

Jaclyn's beast was starting to recover; a surge of power lashed out from her at my words. "You don't know what you're asking, Alec. The cats will wreak nine kinds of destruction."

Tasha was finally meeting my gaze, but the fear that had replaced the hate I'd seen when she'd first arrived wasn't any kind of improvement. I tore my eyes away from her and shook my head at her mother.

"I know exactly what I'm proposing. The Coun'hij pretend to be some kind of benevolent dictatorship, but the truth is that they have left the border packs more or less on their own and you're paying the price for all of those years of neglect. I'm not going to force anyone to my side, but I'm not going to continue propping up a system that is grinding us away like this. The Las Cruces pack will be relocating within a few weeks and once that happens it's only a matter of time before the Carlsbad pack throws their lot in with me."

The horror in Jaclyn's expression hadn't left but she was too smart to be doing anything other than following the chain of logic I was setting out. "The border will leak like a sieve. The humans are struggling just to deal with the drug gangs, they'll be routed once the cats start crossing over en masse. The second-tier packs aren't even close to ready to deal with that kind of combat. They'll join you in droves just to keep from being swept away."

I nodded. It wasn't something I was looking forward to, but it was long past time to call the Coun'hij's bluff. They would either step in and start to limit the damage or our entire race would finally be forced to choose sides.

"It will be tough on the Tucson pack, but it doesn't have to be that way. You can join me. We'll hire security guards to keep an eye on your homes and you can relocate further north."

"You don't have to do this, Alec. Bring your people down to the border and help us push further south. Show everyone that you're a king in the old tradition."

"I can't do that, Jaclyn. I would like to see that cesspool cleaned up as much as anyone. Dominic is proof of the fact that not every cat is a murdering thug, but helping her people has to wait until I've put *our* house in order."

Tasha's anger finally boiled over. "So everyone who has kept the cats from ripping through your tender hides has to leave their homes while you sit here in your pretty little mansion?"

I shook my head, sincerely sorry that things had gotten so bad between Tasha and me. "We won't be staying here either. I'm serious when I say that I won't prop up the current system. The Sanctuary pack will move north too. If I have my way then every single pack in North America will either join me or they'll feel the full weight of what you've dealt with for so many centuries."

It was Jaclyn's turn again to try and dissuade me from my chosen path. "What if you can't put that genie back in the bottle, Alec? Once the cats get a taste for the U.S. you're going to have a hell of a time pushing them back down into Mexico."

"They should disperse as they come north. We'll have a fight on our hands, but the real difficulty will be identifying them. Once we track one down I'll send in kill teams. You and Grayson should be capable of taking out nearly any cat, especially if I back you up with picked teams."

"And if you're wrong? The only thing that has allowed us to stand against them for the last few centuries is the fact that they spend most of their time and energy fighting each other. If they see the weakness at the border as their grand chance to defeat us and come up in greater numbers than you anticipate, then you'll be looking at another great war."

"It's a risk that has to be run. The alternative is to allow the Coun'hij to run us all into the ground over the next few centuries."

There was fire in Jaclyn's eyes, but when we locked gazes she was the first one to look away. "I understand your position. Will you answer two questions for me?"

"Yes, if it's in my power to do so without betraying an oath to someone else."

"What about Tasha?"

Tasha opened her mouth as if to protest, but her mother stared her down. I waited until Jaclyn looked back at me and then nodded.

"I've always understood that your primary concern is for your people, Jaclyn. Believe it or not, I can empathize with your worries about Tasha's future. Rachel is in a similar position in many respects. If you throw your lot in with me then I'll put Tasha on my advisory council. I'm already starting to enforce a slightly artificial power structure here, one based on loyalty and intelligence in addition to who's the best killer. I can't promise to put Tasha at the top of the food chain, but as long as I'm alive I'll make sure that she's off limits when it comes to the petty dominance games she'd otherwise be subjected to."

I could see that Jaclyn was about to protest, but I got the rest of my statement out before she could say anything.

"More importantly, I'll clear the way for Tasha to rise based on her loyalty and intelligence. Ash is even weaker than Tasha, but he sits at my right hand because he gives me good advice and I know that I can count on him when things get rough. I'm dedicated to bringing down the Coun'hij, but I'd like to make other changes along the way. The moonborn are never going to be fit for human-style civilization, but it's past time for us to take a few steps in that direction."

I was pretty sure I'd won her over with that statement. It was too close to what she was trying to accomplish inside of her own pack for it not to resonate with her. I'd always had respect for Jaclyn's aims, it had just been Tasha's callousness that had bothered me.

"I think that I could live with that, Alec. It's not the position I would have chosen for Tasha, but in some ways it might be better for her in the long run than what I'd originally planned. She'd still have access to the family wealth and finally be in a position to rise on her own merits, despite never having manifested a hybrid form."

"Do we have a deal then?"

"Not quite. I'm concerned about your judgment in a few areas. Most important is these dispossessed wolves you've accepted oaths from."

"All of them or someone in particular?"

Jaclyn gave me a grim smile. "What do you think?"

It was a test, but I was going to face much worse before all was said and done. I expressed silent thanks once again for Adri and Shawn as I walked over to one of the two wall vaults behind Donovan's desk.

It was apparently past time for me to get an office of my own, but up until now I'd always made do with using Donovan's office anytime I needed to stash something. I was the only one who knew the combination to this particular lock and Donovan's office had always been the most secure room in the estate.

I spun the massive dial and listened to the complex mechanism and the clicking of the tumblers. The design was my father's. Shape shifter hearing was so good as to make normal combination locks questionable so he'd designed a lock that had dozens of tumblers that dropped into place at random intervals. With all of that noise it was almost impossible to hear the real mechanism operate.

I fished Adri's folder out of the top shelf and leafed through it until I found the pictures of the two submissive wolves who had arrived a few minutes before Grayson.

"These two can't be trusted. They are very good liars, but they didn't mean a word of the oath they swore to me last week. I'll be very careful to keep them away from anything important, and as soon as I have a few more like them I'll use the group for assignments that they can't mess up, probably werewolf hunts, but I'm open to other ideas if you've got any."

I pulled the photos of Grayson, Wyatt and Carson out of the file and dropped them on the desk where Jaclyn could get at them. "These three are a mystery. They refused to swear an oath of fealty to me, but then proceeded to swear something even more binding except that it's time-bounded."

"The question is whether or not you can believe their oath."

"I can trust them. Only until the time limit they agreed to runs out, but I can trust them."

Jaclyn shook her head. "There's no way to really know that, Alec. I've seen some exceptional liars in my time."

"I can't tell you how I know, Jaclyn, but I do. I have a method for detecting lies that involves something other than just listening to someone's heart rate and detecting when their body temperature starts to fluctuate."

"You're serious."

"Absolutely. I can trust these three more than any of those idiots who are still jockeying for position as they throw their daughters at me in the hopes that I'll lose interest in Adri. No, there are plenty of questions still around Grayson and his fellows, but I trust them to do what they're told and not to leak our secrets."

"What *are* you worried about then?"

It was my turn to test her. "Why don't you tell me what you think I should be worried about with regards to them?"

"Fine. This Grayson has always kept a low profile. I always assumed he was just another dispossessed until I started hearing rumors that he had some kind of superpower."

"He does. I watched him send more than a dozen wolves into uncontrollable convulsions. He completely neutralized some very powerful hybrids but left his friends untouched."

Jaclyn went a little white. It had to be hard on her to find out that there was yet another person out there who could take her down before she could get close enough for her ability to kick in.

"It's hard to believe, but it's not any more powerful than what you just did to me. He'd be able to kill whomever he pleases at any time."

I shrugged. "The process seemed to take a lot out of him. He went into convulsions himself, but they weren't as bad. I expect he could probably kill one or two people before he exhausts himself and depletes his ability, but I suspect that he'll really shine when he's got backup. In a larger-scale fight he can drop the other side for a few critical seconds while whoever is with him dispatches them all."

"You're sure about that?"

"No, but when he tested me I...got a feel, for lack of a better term, for his power. I don't think it operates by blanketing an area. I think he targets individuals, even individuals that he can't see. It actually makes him more valuable in a fight than I am. I can't narrow my focus down that far. I can drop an opposing force but I'd have to personally kill everyone I'd dropped."

Jaclyn's eyes lit up. "But his power is ineffective against you?"

"Correct. Assuming he has the brains to match, he'd be the perfect lieutenant. Incredibly deadly, but still submissive to me."

Jaclyn rubbed her hands together slowly and then looked back up at me. "The biggest question is who these three are already sworn to."

"Exactly. It's the logical reason for their inability to swear to me and it could be incredibly significant. There's a whole other power bloc out there that none of the rest of us know about and whoever is in charge is powerful enough that they're even more deadly than Grayson. If I can bring them around to our side they could alter the whole balance of power between us and the Coun'hij."

Tasha looked uneasy, but she finally joined back in the conversation. "What kind of group as powerful as these guys seem to be would just sit out the last couple of hundred years given everything that the Coun'hij has done recently?"

I pulled out the last picture of Grayson, the one where Shawn had zoomed in on the circle of scar tissue on his chest, and dropped it on the table next to the others.

"I don't know, but this is our first clue."

Chapter 8

Adriana Paige
Graves Estate
Sanctuary, Utah

Kami and Rachel hit it off immediately. If the Graves family fortune ever evaporated I was pretty sure that Rachel could make a very good living as a wedding planner. Alec had mentioned hiring help with the wedding, but I'd still been a little surprised when Kami had been ushered into the main library by Donovan.

Less than five minutes after Kami handed me her elegant white business card, she and Rachel were lost inside Rachel's wedding binders. It took half an hour before the two of them surfaced enough to fill me in, but it turned out that Kami wholeheartedly endorsed everything Rachel was doing, she just thought we needed to change up our priorities slightly.

An hour later we were touring different parts of the estate looking for a suitable location for the ceremony. It would have been impossible to cover the kind of ground we needed to cross on foot, but luckily Alec and Rachel's garage was stocked with a host of four-wheeled ATV's in various shapes and sizes.

Rachel had gotten a topographical map from Donovan and then we'd set off on our scouting expedition. Only 'we' included way more than just Rachel, Kami and I. Kristin's attack dream hadn't turned out to be a legitimate precognitive warning, but had caused Alec to reassess security around the estate. I now had at least one bodyguard with me anytime we left the house.

Today it was two and I was starting to feel more than a little claustrophobic. Jasmin wasn't too bad, but I didn't know Carson very well so it felt awkward to have him sitting next to me as Jasmin drove our ATV.

Rachel and Kami's vehicle was being driven by Jess while Carson's friend, Wyatt, ranged around us on a smaller ATV. I knew that Wyatt was trustworthy because Shawn had vouched for the intentions behind the oath Wyatt had sworn to Alec. Even so, it was hard to believe he was very reliable with the way he was darting all over the place.

We came over a small rise as Kami checked the map again and then as we reached the bottom of a bowl-shaped depression she asked Jess to stop. Rachel jumped out of the vehicle before it had completely stopped moving and bounded over to me.

"What do you think, Adri? There are a couple of other places that could work, but I think this one has the most potential."

I looked around at the brown, dying vegetation and the sharp rocks and shrugged. "It's kind of desolate, isn't it?"

Kami smiled at me as she made her way over at a slightly more sedate pace. "You're right, as it is right now you wouldn't want to use it, but look more at the underlying shape of the ground and try to think about what it could look like. Here, let me show you."

I dutifully followed as she took me on a guided tour of what she would do with the bowl if 'money was no object.' At first it was really hard to see the transformation she was talking about, but as time went on I started to be able to see it.

The bowl would be deepened slightly to create a natural amphitheater and then graded and covered in sod. We'd transplant hedges up onto the rim of the bowl to create a windbreak and shield the park we were creating from outside view. There'd be a fountain on one end, just behind where we'd stand for the ceremony, with flowerbeds interspersed throughout the park full of whatever flowers I chose.

Kami and Rachel were a matched pair. Ideas flowed out of them in a torrent that got more overwhelming the longer I listened to it.

"I generally try to make sure that any proposed locations can handle inclement weather. Luckily that wouldn't be too difficult here. I think the best bet would be some decorative arches or something else similar that could be used to support some kind of canopy if the weather turned bad."

Rachel was literally bouncing up and down. Sometime over the last couple of days she'd become even more energetic. It was like she was in danger of starting on fire if she didn't stay in motion at all times. "That's a great idea, but would you do one big canopy or lots of small ones?"

Kami looked at me but I just shrugged. I was still a little shocked that I was actually considering buying off on the idea in the first place. Alec was going to be paying a small fortune to the local landscapers to have any chance of pulling this off in two months.

"A single big canopy would be the simplest, but it would require a very tall pole in the center to work. My suggestion would be to set up a series of smaller zones that are designed to be covered with smaller canopies. The real difficulty is in making sure that the guests can move back and forth between zones without getting drenched. Decorative arches where the canopies meet would solve that problem nicely."

Rachel nodded in double-time. "Then you just need to deal with the water running off of the canopies. Maybe a system of tiny streams that mostly match up with the zones?"

Kami nodded. "Yes, I think that would be best. Possibly linked to the fountain in some form or fashion. The streams wouldn't have to exactly match up with the edges of the canopy, you just need the areas that the canopy is covering to be elevated enough that the water will run off into the channels rather than back at your guests."

I felt like my mind was betraying me, but I could see it now. A series of tiny streams crisscrossing the amphitheater with functional bridges spanning them. The canopy idea wasn't bad either. I could even see sections where a covered walkway would bridge the distance between canopies.

"Remind me again, dear, how many people are you planning on having attend?"

I looked at Rachel because I had no idea. I already knew that there were going to be more people than I would have invited, but I didn't know exactly how big that number was likely to be.

"Mom and Dad sent out more than six hundred invitations. Given Alec's recent rise in...prominence...I expect you guys will be inviting somewhere in the neighborhood of a thousand guests."

I suddenly felt like I needed to sit down. The thought of a thousand people watching me stumble my way up to the altar was enough to make me sick. Rachel saw my expression and gave me a reassuring smile as she distracted Kami with questions about how we'd get a thousand guests out to this part of the estate.

As the two of them walked away, still talking, I picked out a large rock and sat down. Wyatt watched them go and then shook his head. "Seems like an awful lot of fuss for no reason."

Jess rolled her eyes at him. "It's a girl thing, you've probably never even thought about what your wedding would be like."

"Sure I have. It's going to be a theme wedding. The ushers will be dressed like vampires, we'll have werewolves on the cake and her family will all have to come wearing cat costumes."

Jess looked at Wyatt like he'd grown a second head for a second and then burst out laughing. It was nice to see her so relaxed, but the two of them were starting to give me a headache. Carson gave me a considering look and then pointed at Rachel. "It's kind of hard for the two of you to protect Rachel from all of the way over here."

Wyatt sighed and then turned and started trudging off in Rachel's direction with Jess only a couple of steps behind.

Jasmin rubbed her temples. "Bloody brilliant. I thought they'd never shut up. Now if you can just figure out a way to keep two football fields between us and Rachel at all times we'll all have a chance of hearing ourselves think."

Jasmin was more than capable of being prickly, but this felt like more than just her normal frustration at having to change her plans at the last minute.

"Are you okay, Jas?"

I caught a quick look at Carson before Jasmin nodded and then turned away as if the discussion was over. Fortunately, Carson caught the look.

"I think I see something over on that ridge that needs checked out. Jasmin, if you can stay next to Adri then I'll just go over and have a look."

Jasmin nodded and then we waited until Carson was out of earshot before she sighed. "Sorry, I shouldn't be so snippy, I'm just having a hard time dealing right now."

"With the Ben thing?"

Even as I said it I felt a surge of guilt. I'd only visited Ben a couple of times since we'd flown back from Chicago. Jasmin had knocked him unconscious when she'd been extricating him from the vampire-run auto body shop where he'd been working. Alec had flown in several specialists and everyone was in agreement that the damage from the head blow had long since healed, but Ben still hadn't regained consciousness.

"Yeah. Ben's part of it, but in some ways, that's actually the easiest part. As long as Ben is still asleep then I don't have to worry about where we stand. We don't exactly have a very smooth history together, so it's possible that him still being unconscious is the only thing saving me from another round of disappointment."

I hadn't quite thought of things in that light. I was pretty sure that Ben had been ready to finally give Jasmin the chance she deserved, but given some of the water under the bridge I could understand her reluctance to believe that he wasn't going to just run away again.

"So Ben's only part of it then. What's the rest?"

"It's this crap with Alec still. You remember our talk in New York? The thing I'd lost because of Alec?"

She was referring to the speed and strength advantage that all of the descendants of the royal line got. Apparently it was a closely guarded secret, enough so that she wasn't willing to explicitly mention it, even with Carson being so far away.

Jasmin checked my expression to make sure that I knew what she was talking about and then shrugged. "I thought that maybe I'd get it back. You know, now that Alec isn't subconsciously draining us all of the time. I'm not tired all of the time anymore, none of us are, but that thing that I lost is still gone."

All of a sudden some of Jasmin's irritability was making a lot more sense than it had previously. I was still feeling my way through so much of what it meant to be part of the pack, but I knew that this was a big deal.

I didn't necessarily like the fact that the strongest members of the pack got to order the weaker members of the pack around, but it was a fact of life at this point. Alec never let the dominants get away with some of the excesses that I heard about in other packs, but it still meant that the hybrids were king and the wolves who couldn't manifest a third shape were peasants. I knew that Alec was working to change that, but even if he succeeded it wouldn't alter the fact that Jasmin was a shadow of what she'd been previously.

Even if nobody was ordering her around she was still less capable of defending herself than she'd been before Alec's power had stripped away her 'royal wolf' abilities. Given that we were on the brink of a war with the Coun'hij, it was more than likely that Jasmin would find herself on the frontlines at some point.

"I'm sorry, Jasmin. I didn't know. I never even considered the fact that you might have lost...that thing...permanently."

Jasmin shrugged, but I knew her well enough now to know that the movement was part of the perfect mask that she presented to the world. Jasmin's incredible beauty was just another part of her arsenal. Her gorgeous dark hair and perfectly symmetrical features were as much a weapon as the fangs of her wolf form. She used all of it to keep the world at arm's length.

"There isn't anything to be done about it now. I need to just accept that this is how things are going to be from now on and move on with my life."

Maybe, but to me that sounded more like a recipe for her becoming more and more bitter as time went on.

"Have you talked to Alec about everything?"

"No. There's nothing he can do about it at this point and he's got a lot of other things on his mind now."

I found myself sighing. I was really, really bad at girl talk. "Maybe you're right that this is just how things are going to be in the future, but I think that you're doing him a real disservice by not telling him. He would want to know what you've sacrificed to keep the pack safe."

Jasmin shrugged again, but I was pretty sure that I'd finally gotten through to her. She waved at Carson and then we spent the couple of minutes required for him to return in silence.

As Carson walked back towards us I noticed a difference in his manner. I wanted to say that he was more relaxed, but that wasn't the right word. He was more...centered. He took a deep breath as he reached us and then smiled at me.

"I know it's not my place to interfere with your wedding plans, but I have some experience with gardens. I expect that Alec will keep me too busy to actually help with the planting of everything, but if you'd like to share your colors with me I'd be happy to plan the arrangement of the gardens here."

It was an odd offer, but I didn't want to offend him with an ill-thought-out response. I considered my words for several seconds and then gave him a smile.

"I appreciate the offer, Carson. You're welcome to help if you'd like, but I'm sure that Kami has people who can do all of that if your time would be better spent doing something else."

Carson nodded. "I'm sure that she has people who are very good at planning a visual display of flowers, but I'm equally positive that none of them are my match when it comes to scents. If you're going to truly impress your moonborn guests then you'll need both. This place already has a healthy smell to it. It shouldn't be too hard to turn it into something worthy of your special day."

Jasmin looked as shocked as I was, but I didn't have to think twice. "More than just accepting your offer, I am profoundly grateful for it. I would be honored to have you plan that part of the occasion and, unless I'm very mistaken, I think I have a secret weapon for you that you're going to appreciate more than almost anyone else could." I could see that I'd intrigued Carson, but he merely bowed his head slightly in agreement before turning to watch Rachel and Kami's progress back towards us. Jess and Wyatt walked a couple of steps behind Rachel, but even I could see that they were talking too much to be paying any attention to their charge.

The quartet was less than a dozen feet away from us when Jess shot her foot between Wyatt's legs, tripping him in spectacular fashion. Wyatt was fast though and managed to get a hand on Jess and take her with him.

As the two of them hit the ground and rolled, I momentarily thought that they were about to break out into a dominance fight. It wasn't until they came to a stop with Jess on top that I realized they were both laughing.

Carson's expression was grim, but I suspected that mine was just as unhappy. Carson was probably frustrated by the fact that Wyatt wasn't holding up his end of things as a bodyguard. I was worried about something even more important than that. Jess was flirting with Wyatt, and while I was glad that she was starting to regain her mental and emotional footing, this was really going to piss Isaac off.

Chapter 9

Alec Graves
Graves Estate
Sanctuary, Utah

Jasmin was in one of her moods again. I could feel her staring daggers into my back as she followed me down the hall. I'd tried to tease whatever it was out of her several times over the last couple of weeks, but so far she'd refused to open up.

This was a terrible time to try and resolve whatever the issue was. I was supposed to be at another reception in five minutes so that I could take oaths from all of the new arrivals, but I was starting to realize that there would never be a good time to take care of it. Jasmin was either a priority or she wasn't. If she was, then I needed to treat her like one.

I double-checked our location in the house and tried to remember if we'd put any of the new arrivals in this wing or not. I didn't think so, but honestly it was nearly a full-time job to keep track of all of the visitors. I finally just shrugged, took Jasmin by the arm and led her into one of the bedrooms. If it turned out to be occupied then whoever was there would just have to forgive the intrusion. It was my house after all.

I flipped on the white noise generator and then faced Jasmin again. "Okay, Jas, spill it. What's wrong?"

"I don't know what you're talking about, Alec. We need to get moving or you're going to be late for your precious meeting."

"Come on, this is me. I'd know you were lying even if your pulse hadn't just shot up. What has you so pissed off?"

"Okay, Alec. You want to know? I'll tell you what has me so pissed off. It's you. Ever since you manifested your power you don't think about how any of this will impact our pack. You're so busy taking care of Rebekka, Louis and the rest that you don't have any time for me and the others."

I opened my mouth to tell her that she was wrong, but she talked over the top of me. "Ben is getting weaker, but you've got me serving as some kind of bullcrap honor guard instead of spending my time with him like I want to."

That shut me up, at least for a moment. I waited to see what else Jasmin would say, but she seemed to have said everything she was going to say.

"I'm sorry, Jasmin. I didn't know Ben's condition was deteriorating. Why didn't you say something sooner?"

"You get copied on all of the reports I see. You ought to at least, since you're the one that's footing the bill."

"I get sent more than eight hundred pages of reports each day. I have to pick and choose what I read. I figured that you'd come find me if there was something I needed to be aware of in his workups."

Jasmin still looked like she mostly wanted to take a swing at me but she'd relaxed slightly. "Well, I didn't think I should have to."

I realized I was rubbing the side of my head and made myself stop. The stress headaches were getting worse, but that didn't mean that I could go around showing everyone that I was only days away from falling apart.

"I asked you to stand behind me today because I was trying to elevate your importance. The more people see you as having my ear the less crap they should give you because they'll be worried about how I'll respond."

"I guess I just wanted to actually have your ear rather than just the appearance of you trusting me."

My beast seemed harder than ever to control these days, but I tightened up its leash and kept my tone as reasonable as I could.

"If you want to be one of my advisors I'm fine with that. I've been trying to give you time and space because I knew you wanted to be with Ben. You've got the same problem I have right now, Jas. You can't have it both ways, you have to choose between priorities."

It was like I'd hit her. She didn't move for several seconds and then finally looked up at me and nodded. "You're right. I can't have it both ways. The truth is that isn't the only thing that's bothering me."

"Out with it, Jas."

"I lost my royal wolf attributes, Alec. I'm no different than Jess."

It was my turn to reel away from the impact of what she'd just said. "Are you sure?"

"Yeah. I only jump about two-thirds as far as I used to."

There was only one logical cause and my throat closed up as I realized that it had been me who had robbed Jasmin of part of her heritage.

"I'm sorry, Jas. I didn't know what I was doing back then."

"I know. I've been telling myself that for weeks now, but it's still hard to deal with. I kept hoping that it was just the aftereffects of the exhaustion from when you were unconsciously draining us, but it looks like it's permanent."

I cast about for a solution, but there wasn't one. I could put her under the same kind of protection as Rachel and Adri, but she was too proud to ever agree to that. Jasmin read my thoughts from the expression on my face and mustered a smile as she patted my arm.

"It's okay, Alec. I was willing to follow you back when I thought it was going to result in my death. This is hardly a fate worse than death. It's going to take some time, but I'll work through my crap eventually. In the grand scheme of things, my sacrifice is a pretty small one to help ensure that the pack survived."

"That doesn't make it any easier."

"No, you're right, it doesn't. I think you were right though when you said earlier that I need to prioritize. I've been spending too much time moping at Ben's bedside. Give me a job, something that will keep me busy for three or four hours a day and take my mind off of everything that's gone wrong in the last six months."

"It's a deal. Give me a couple of days to decide where you'll do the most good, but I promise I'll make it a priority. I always need an intelligent mind that I can trust to help filter out the stuff that is important from the stuff that isn't."

Ten minutes later we were inside the reception hall. Jasmin took a place at my back with Ash standing next to her. Louis had been forced to fly back to New Mexico for a few days, but Rebekka was there standing proudly in a place of honor on the other side of Ash.

Grayson was manning the main entrance with one of Ulrich's hybrids, a stocky specimen who went by the handle of Ace, backing him up. Ulrich hadn't technically sworn fealty to me, but he was in this up to his neck, so he'd agreed to keep a few people here under my command as extra guards.

I suspected that he was using it as a way of getting people who were causing him problems out of his pack for a little while, but that was okay. Ulrich sometimes had to resort to bribery to deal with some of the more dangerous members of the Chicago pack but I didn't have that problem. I could safely stare down any of his people if push came to shove.

I was however trying very hard these days not to have to use my power, which was where Grayson came in. Until I could get Jaclyn to join me, Grayson would continue to be my strongest weapon. Even after she joined there were still going to be instances where he was the better tool for a given job.

With Grayson standing quietly on one side of the door my odds of having to use my power dropped drastically and he was an enormous force multiplier. Even if every new arrival were to attack us all at once, Grayson would be able to neutralize them for the few minutes Ash,

Jasmin and Rebekka would need to kill everyone in the room.

The first few delegations were a combination of new arrivals and individuals who'd fled when Kristin had warned that we were going to come under attack. We now had representatives from more than a dozen states, but everyone in this batch was jockeying for position, looking for an alliance rather than binding themselves to me like I needed them to.

Ash announced the last of the new arrivals and I suppressed a sigh of relief as they approached the elevated dais where I was sitting. I only had to make it through another fifteen minutes of semi-useless ceremony and then I'd be able to get back to doing the things that I really needed to be doing.

My relief lasted only until I got a good look at the blonde girl my age who trailed half a step behind the head of the delegation. She was gorgeous in a way that only few women ever achieved. I watched as the eye of every single male in the room gravitated towards her.

I'd grown up around beautiful females, but there was something about this girl that put all others of her kind to shame. She gave me a smile that was somehow shy and assertive at the same time as she took two steps forward, putting herself at the front of her delegation.

"We thank you for welcoming us into your pack's territory. We are prepared to uphold all of the traditional duties of a guest and I place myself at your service to answer any questions you might have."

Something about the way she looked up at me from underneath dark lashes implied that she was eager to do more than just answer questions. An almost overwhelming wave of desire crashed through me, but the very strength of the emotion felt wrong. I loved Adri with all of my heart, but I knew what had gone into our relationship reaching the point it was currently at.

We'd faced down certain death together, we'd spent countless hours talking, sharing things with each other that we'd never told anyone else. It was impossible for me to want anyone else as badly as I wanted Adri, not when I'd just met that someone else, not when I didn't even know her name.

"I'm afraid that we haven't been introduced yet..."

I was stalling for time. The very act of realizing that something felt wrong about my feelings towards this girl helped clear my head slightly, but I could only think of one route forward. I nodded as she told me that her name was Lori, but my attention was focused on taking the chains off of my ability.

It was harder than I'd expected to get my power to activate, but I was pretty sure that the difficulties were all mental. A second later a tiny rift opened up and my eyes went wide as I was finally able to detect her power at work.

It was so incredibly subtle that I almost couldn't believe that I'd managed to avoid being taken in by her. Delicate tendrils of power reached out from her to nearly every person in the room. They were burrowing into each of us and artificially creating the attraction that I'd felt.

I opened the rift up more widely, just enough to make the tendrils between her and me disintegrate, and then looked back up to find that she'd closed the distance between us. Some of the tendrils that had been touching other people were drifting my way now. It meant that there was only a tendril or two touching the others, but it didn't seem to be making any difference. Everyone else in the room was firmly in her thrall.

Lori was beautiful, that much hadn't been artificial. Even now, with exhaustion starting to show at the corners of her eyes, I was impressed with just how flawless she was physically. She didn't seem to know that I'd shaken off her power. Instead of pulling back and pretending nothing had happened, she was leaning in even closer, a sultry smile on her face as the additional tendrils she was sending my way momentarily grew fat with power before touching me and then disintegrating.

She reached out and placed a hand on my chest, and for a moment the attraction was back.

There was no subtlety this time, it was a tsunami of lust and the shock of the feelings was enough to make me open my rift far enough that she dropped to the ground in front of me.

Her father manifested his hybrid form instantly and moved forward. I didn't know whether he was attacking me or merely trying to protect his daughter, but ultimately it didn't matter. I opened my ability even wider but kept it centered on the two of them. They were a powerful pair and I felt the other end of the conduit protest at the amount of power being funneled into it. I knew I was taking a risk, that the smart thing would be for me to let Grayson take over immobilizing the two of them, but it was past time to make a point to those watching me.

Always before I'd simply relaxed my grip on my ability and it had done what needed doing. This time I reached out and pulled, channeling more and more of Lori and her father's power into the singularity.

The absorption field started to wobble, but I kept it up by pure force of will as I pulled even harder. A tremor started in my legs, but I managed to prolong the situation for two more seconds before the rift collapsed.

Lori was an unhealthy white, unmoving but for the rise and fall of her chest, but it was the sight of her father that had everyone in the room staring in shock. They hadn't seen me force

Jaclyn back into her human form, but this was more even than that. The unnatural vitality of our kind had failed him. Instead of pulling himself back to his feet like the proud alpha he was, her father was still collapsed on the floor, gasping for breath as though the mere act of breathing was almost more than he could handle.

I let my 'guests' take in the extent of my power for nearly a full minute before I looked back at Jasmin and Ash. "Get two cages. They came here with the intention of using her ability on me. They violated guest right before they even arrived. Send them back to Del Rio in cages as an example of what happens to those who abuse my hospitality."

Lori managed to roll over onto her back and look up at me. "Please don't do this. They'll tear us apart now that they know what I've been doing to them all this time."

I didn't want to send her back. Looking at her lying helpless on the floor, it was all I could do to not to rescind the order. I would have blamed her ability, but I was confident that she was too exhausted to play those kinds of games right now.

"You've left me no choice. I can't trust you here even if I was inclined to do so after what you've just done. Maybe it's time that you face justice for enslaving so many."

I stood there for the fifteen minutes it took for the cages to arrive unoccupied and then disappear from the room with Lori and her father in them. Nobody said a word until I returned to my seat and sat down.

Raynor was the first to speak up. "Do you have your temper back under control enough that you're willing to listen to reason?"

It was all that I could do not to move around in my chair, and my beast felt the same way. He paced back and forth inside the corner of my mind where I normally kept him captive. In a way it was probably a good thing that Raynor chose to speak. It gave us both a target for the energy that was coursing through us.

"I rarely refuse to listen to reason. I don't, however, remember giving you permission to address me in such a manner. You're my guest here and like it or not, I'm dominant to you. If you have something useful to say then say it, but mind your manner."

Raynor looked up at me with the eyes of his beast showing through. "Do you really think that you can continue to insult us all? Since the day we arrived you've done nothing but put us off. At every turn you've refused to give us adequate time to discuss the business that brought us here."

"I'm no different than you, Raynor. I have to prioritize my time where it will do the most good."

"You've prioritized it towards weaklings like Rebekka and Louis. If you were anyone else I'd never have stood for your ridiculous choice to put those two above the rest of us. They bring nothing to the table while I bring the second largest pack in North America as a bargaining chip."

Raynor had stalked towards me while he spoke. I could see that Grayson was on hair trigger, but I waved him back and instead stood and stepped forward until I was only inches away from Raynor.

"I'm not looking to marry your daughter, Raynor. If you want to join me, then join me, but you're not going to get some kind of alliance of equals out of me, especially not by way of marriage."

A growl bubbled up out of him, but my beast responded with a surge of power that caused a few of those watching to take a step back.

"Rebekka and Louis can be depended upon. They bring loyalty to the table. I don't care what else you might bring to the table; until you've proven your loyalty to me, you'll always be less to me than they will."

Raynor shook his head. "The strongest always have the place of honor."

"I am the strongest here and I'll choose who I honor. The days of might being the sole criteria are over. Loyalty will always trump ability for me."

"You're trying to turn all of us into mere subjects?"

"There is no such thing as a 'mere' subject, not to me. Those who've sworn allegiance to me are the most important. I refuse to neglect those to whom I have a mutual bond of loyalty in order to chase after possibilities. You will either join me or you won't. I'm willing to let you make your own choices—do you really think that the Coun'hij will do the same? For them there have only ever been two kinds of people. Those who are with them, and those who aren't. Your 'neutrality' won't be worth anything when things actually start to heat up."

Whatever Raynor might have said was preempted by Dominic's arrival.

"Alec, come quick! It's Rachel, she's gone crazy."

Chapter 10

Adriana Paige
Graves Estate
Sanctuary, Utah

Alec called me on his way to Rachel's room so I arrived there, with Carson hot on my heels, only a minute or so after he got there. Donovan, and Dominic were both there already and everyone looked just as upset as I felt. Rachel had seemed like she was fully back to normal for the last little while. It just didn't seem fair for her to be having problems now, not after everything she'd been through since Alec's power had first started manifesting.

"I've called Dr. Samuels. I don't expect that he'll know what to do, but he can at least put us in touch with the relevant specialists."

Alec nodded in response to Donovan but his gaze was fixed on Rachel, who was twirling about in the center of her room. It was a normal enough kind of scene until you took in the ruined pillows and the heaps of feathers strewn about on the carpet around her. As I watched, Rachel started jumping into the air, grabbing at something that wasn't actually there.

I opened and closed my mouth a couple of times in an effort to say something comforting, but there wasn't anything that could make what we were seeing be anything other than terrible.

Alec watched Rachel jump for several minutes before he walked over and gently guided her into her favorite chair, the one that faced the window. It meant that she was mostly turned away from us, but I had a suspicion that he'd done that on purpose.

As Alec knelt down in front of Rachel she flinched back like she was afraid he was going to hit her. Her hands came up in front of her face and then she looked at Alec with squinting eyes.

"Rachel, can you hear me?"

She dropped her hands and looked at him with her head cocked to the side. Her lips moved silently for several seconds before she blinked rapidly and then nodded. "Of course you do, Alec."

Rachel turned and looked at the empty corners of the room and smiled. "You all do. I hope that you know how much it means to me."

Alec slowly waved his hand in front of Rachel's face, but her stare didn't waver. If she hadn't responded to his question I would have said that we didn't even exist for her.

Jess rushed into the room, skidding to a halt when she saw that Rachel had company. I caught a flash of movement out of the corner of my eye and turned to see who it was, but they disappeared around a corner before I could see anything other than the fact that they were big and male.

Alec looked up at Jess with anger bubbling just under the surface of his eyes. "Where were you?"

"Rachel was in her room working on wedding stuff. I figured since we were inside the house that it wasn't a big deal if I took a break."

"You figured wrong. As long as we have visitors here who haven't sworn fealty to me I want Rachel, Adri, and my mother under a constant guard."

"I deserve to have a life, Alec."

Alec stood up and walked over to Jess as Rachel smiled at the way the sunlight was now hitting her face.

"I'm not going to argue with you, Jess. Because you weren't here we don't know if this was a natural phenomenon or if Rachel was attacked by someone."

Jess looked unsure of herself for the first time in days. It seemed to have finally sunk in for her that Rachel wasn't okay.

"I'm sorry, Alec. I wasn't thinking."

"You're right, you were being an idiot."

Rachel stood back up and twirled around again, picking invisible things out of the air. "Hmm, he's so nice. Takes such good care of me..."

Whatever she said trailed off into something much too quiet for me to hear but it was obvious that Alec heard it all. His fists tightened up until his knuckles were white and then he shook himself.

"You know that we all love you right, Rach?"

Rachel smiled, but I got the impression that she was smiling at the way that the light played on the seat she'd just vacated. Alec gently pulled her into a hug and then looked at Dominic and me. "Can you two watch her until I can make other arrangements?"

We both nodded, which seemed to satisfy him. He squeezed Rachel's arm and started towards the door. Just before he left the room he turned back and looked at Rachel.

"It's going to be okay; we'll figure out how to get through this."

Rachel didn't seem to have heard. Alec sighed and then left with Donovan a couple of steps behind him. Jess looked at Rachel for nearly a minute. She looked a couple of times like she was going to say something, possibly an apology, but she ended up leaving with whatever it was still unsaid.

Dominic gently turned Rachel around and lowered her to the ground. "Let's clean up these pillows, Rachel."

Rachel complied with the order, slowly gathering up feathers and stuffing them into an empty pillowcase. I dropped down to help and between the three of us we made slow but steady progress.

We'd been working for nearly fifteen minutes before Rachel suddenly looked up from her pile of feathers and smiled again. "That's highly unlikely. At least not soon. You have to know what you're up against first."

It made no sense, but it somehow reminded me of the flash of movement that I'd seen with Jess.

"Dom, do you know who was with Jess just now?"

Dom nodded but the motion was hesitant. "It...it was Wyatt. They've been spending a lot of time together lately."

I felt like my head was going to explode and rubbing my temples didn't help at all.

"They were flirting with each other the other day too. I was kind of hoping that it was just my imagination or that it would blow over after a couple of days. Isaac is going to freak out."

Rachel threw a handful of feathers into the air and then plucked them out of it one at a time before patting me on the shoulder. "Don't worry, Adri. Gray is Isaac's favorite color."

Chapter 11

Alec Graves
Graves Estate
Sanctuary, Utah

"I'm telling you, Alec. There are at least half a dozen wolves there who would jump ship if given half a chance. We need to go down to New Orleans in force and get them out of there."

Adri had communicated Ash's request several days ago, but apparently Ash had decided to ignore my gentle hints that now wasn't the time to address this. We were just about to start a briefing meeting which meant that Rebekka and Louis were already there as was Donovan. Jaclyn was supposed to be here within the next half an hour so I really needed to get things moving or we wouldn't be able to cover everything I wanted to talk about before she came strolling into the room.

"I understand where you are coming from, Ash. Believe it or not, I really do, but I can't just go around destabilizing packs right now or I'm going to push anyone who's currently on the fence about joining us right into the opposing camp."

"They want out, Alec. They deserve to get out of there but they won't be able to manage it on their own. That has to mean something to you."

I was exhausted, more than exhausted really. Dr. Samuels had put us in contact with four different specialists, each of whom I'd flown out over the last couple of days, but none of them had any idea what was wrong with Rachel.

Their answer had been to suggest a number of really powerful prescription medications, but I hadn't wanted to put Rachel on anything until I was sure that it wasn't some kind of attack, either by the Coun'hij or one of our guests. I needed to get Mallory back to the estate and have her give all of the new arrivals a once-over to see if they had an unreported power that they were using against Rach, but I hadn't been able to tear myself away from everything else yet to take another trip out to Mallory's cabin.

"Okay, Ash, I'll tell you what. If anyone from that pack communicates with you and tells you that they want out, then I'll take action. It would be better if they called me up and told me directly, but I'll act even if they just talk to you. Until then my hands are tied."

Ash was pacing now. "That will never work. My sister hates your family with a passion. She blames your ancestors for everything that happened to our family. She'd rather die than ask you for help."

"If that's really the case then there isn't anything I can do."

"Onyx is scared, Alec. After what you did to his delegation it's only a matter of time before he throws his lot in completely with the Coun'hij. Once Puppeteer and the rest are keeping an eye on the area we may not get another chance at this."

"I'm not disagreeing with you, Ash, but I'm not the one you need to be trying to convince. Get your sister or someone else in the pack to ask for help and I'll send Grayson down there and we'll get as many of them out as want to go, but you're going to want to make darn sure that your sister is ready to come with us. We're only going to get one shot and if she doesn't come with us when she has the chance then things are going to get really, really bad for her once we are gone."

Ash didn't like my position, but I gave him a look that said we were done talking about the New Orleans pack right now and he finally took the hint and shut up. I waited a second to make sure that he was really done and then turned to Louis and Rebekka.

"I want to start cycling your people through Sanctuary. I know we've done a little bit of that, but I want to speed it up and get all of them here at some point or another during the next two weeks."

Rebekka gave me a funny look. "How come?"

"Your people need to swear fealty so that we know we can trust them. It doesn't have to be to me, I'm not trying to break your packs up necessarily, but they need to swear to you or to someone else in your pack who has sworn to you or to me."

Louis winced slightly. I already knew that he was going to bleed to make that happen, but it was important. I'd been serious about what I'd told Raynor. I needed people I could trust just as badly as I needed capable fighters and brilliant minds.

"I know it's not going to be easy, but there is precedent. Thanatas and Jaldul both enforced an oath of fealty among their supporters."

Rebekka frowned like she was worried how I would respond, but after several seconds she threw her two cents in as well.

"I don't think you realize just how hard it's going to be to get some of our people to swear fealty to anyone. A precedent that ancient isn't going to help very much."

My beast was acting up more than normal lately, but I forced it down. I had to keep control of myself or my people would stop telling me what they really thought.

"I'm not going to force anyone to swear fealty to me or you. I do need to know who we can depend on though. I think given enough time that people will start choosing to join us of their own free will, but before that can happen we're going to need some people already bound to us so that everyone else can see the benefits our people are reaping."

Louis breathed a sigh of relief. "You were serious about what you told Raynor then?"

"Couldn't you tell that I was telling the truth?"

Rebekka answered this time. "I couldn't see any signs of a lie, but it seemed so impossible."

"I meant every word of it. Those of your people who swear fealty will be brought into the inner circle. They won't necessarily sit in this meeting with us, but they will be shown a level of trust that the rest of your people won't be given."

"What about your pack? Have they sworn fealty to you?"

Louis flinched a little when he met my eyes but he didn't retract the question.

"I'm going to have the same problems with some of them that you're going to have with some of your people, but that is the long-term goal."

Donovan spoke up for the first time since we'd all arrived. "I'll take the oath right now if you wish, Master Alec."

"Thank you, Donovan, but I'd like for it to be a public matter. You're welcome to swear to me at the next formal reception."

Ash looked at me defiantly. "I'm not swearing to you."

"I didn't expect that you would, not yet. You still owe an obligation to your sister. Once you've fulfilled that then maybe you'll be willing to take the next step."

I could see a hot retort on the tip of his tongue, but he swallowed it and stood as if to go. I held up a hand. "I do trust you, Ash, and I want you in my councils. Maybe you can come up with a lesser oath that you'd be willing to swear in the meantime, but for today please stay."

I watched as Ash returned to his seat and then opened my mouth to continue with the meeting, but a knock on the door interrupted me.

Donovan opened the door and I waved Jaclyn inside the room. She looked each of the others over for several seconds and then turned back to me. She'd wrapped her pride around herself, but even if the others couldn't see it I could still see just how scared she was. I'd been there myself within the last couple of months.

She'd spent her life protecting her pack and while she'd no doubt made mistakes in the past, they'd been her mistakes to deal with. Putting everything you valued into the hands of another was a terrifying prospect, but even before she opened her mouth I knew that she was going to submit to me.

"I'm here to take your damn oath, Alec."

"Believe it or not, I know what it cost you to come here and say that, Jaclyn. Please take a seat. The actual oath can wait for a couple of days until the next reception, but I know you'll go through with it so I'd like to bring you and everyone else here more fully into my plans."

Each of the members of my inner circle leaned forward slightly. They all knew bits and pieces, but this was their first chance to hear the master plan straight from my lips.

"I want Jaclyn and Louis to start preparing to move their people off of the border. The Las Cruces pack will come here to Sanctuary to live for the next few months while Jaclyn's pack will head to Tonopah. Don't rush your preparations, be smart about arranging for protection for your homes, but we need to make the move happen as soon as is sensible. That will put pressure on the rest of the border packs and the next tier of defenders."

Jaclyn knew this was coming, but it was a complete surprise for Louis. "Some of my people will refuse to go. Just knowing that they are going to be thrown in with another pack will have some of them running scared."

"I know it will, but you're going to need to do everything you can to convince them. I don't want to lose anyone if we can find a way to avoid it. Jaclyn will serve as my enforcer, at least initially, in Tonopah while I'll keep order here in Sanctuary. The goal will be to integrate the power structures of the pack with the minimal amount of disruption possible. People can still challenge each other, but it will happen at scheduled times and those challenges only change the dominance pyramid of the pack to the extent that those involved aren't under orders from me or someone in my power structure."

Jaclyn was nodding now. "The dominants won't like that, but it's not that much more artificial than what I've enforced in Tucson. You'll create an incredible amount of goodwill with the submissives in all three packs. Some of them will swear to you just to get out from under the dominants who have been giving them grief."

"I suspect you're right, but ultimately the goal is to get the dominants to swear an oath as well so that things don't become too unbalanced. Either way though we need to keep any excesses checked. We're going to start running excursions into vampire country and doing werewolf hunts to help keep everyone from losing their edge."

Rebekka looked relieved. "That should prevent things from boiling over. Anytime there is an external threat it goes a long ways towards keeping the dominants from beating on the rest of the pack too much."

"Agreed. Is that something that you can all live with?"

I waited until everyone had nodded, and then handed them each a folder. "I wish that was the only set of marching orders that I had for today. That alone would be plenty to keep us all busy, but I also need you to start working on this."

Jaclyn read the first paragraph and then snorted. "You can't be serious, Alec. Really, the ghost pack? It's just one of those urban legends."

I held up a hand before anyone else could join in. "I know what you're thinking. Rumors of a super-pack have abounded for years but nobody has ever come back with anything concrete on them. Our recent arrivals have gotten me thinking though. Grayson has kept his head down for years despite the fact that he could have easily taken over nearly any pack in North America. That all by itself would have been an oddity, but now we find out that he's sworn to someone or something else. The ghost pack is rumored to be made up of some of the most unique hybrids ever born and they are said to be protected by an alpha who is nearly unbeatable in combat. What if Grayson is that alpha?"

Donovan and Ash had been the two to pull together the briefing on everything we knew or suspected about the ghost pack, but I could see that even they hadn't made the possible connection.

I continued on, building my case point by point. "Grayson has some kind of permanent circle on his chest and we've confirmed that

Wyatt and Carson both have the same kind of distinguishing mark on them. They are obviously part of some kind of group and they are feeling us out right now, evaluating whether or not they want to come out of the shadows and offer us some kind of alliance."

Louis chewed on his lip as he considered what I'd just said. "Why not just wait for them to finish their evaluation before we get too wrapped up in looking for them?"

"Several reasons actually. Knowledge is power—the more I know about them the better off we'll be. They may not even be people that we want to align ourselves with when all is said and done, but it's much better for me to know that before we get into serious discussions with them. Also, there's no guarantee that Grayson is part of the ghost pack. If one group of powerful wolves has managed to stay hidden for centuries then there's no reason to believe that there couldn't be other groups that we don't know about."

Ash flipped to the very last page and held it up. "Any set of wolves would represent an asset against the Coun'hij, but that's not why you're after them, is it? You want this one, don't you?"

I nodded as everyone flipped back to the page Ash was referring to. "You're right. If there really is a hybrid out there who can find other wolves across long distances then he or she represents our best solution for finding the Coun'hij and wiping out their base."

If they'd been shocked before, now they were dumbfounded. They'd been thinking solely in terms of defense because nobody knew where the Coun'hij were based. I'd spent plenty of time thinking about how I was going to defend my people and I'd come to the unfortunate realization that unless we were able to get much more concentrated than we were now, there was no way to guarantee that we wouldn't go down the first time that Puppeteer sent in a pack of werewolves.

I couldn't afford the luxury of letting the Coun'hij call all of the shots. I needed to find a way to bring the fight to them and fast.

Jaclyn was the first to recover and her smile didn't exactly light up the room, but it had a certain air of aggressive satisfaction to it that I liked. "You're right. If you can find them then they won't last half an hour against us. Not with you, Grayson and me. Unless Puppeteer has dozens of werewolves nearby for security we'd tear through them like paper."

"Yes, as things stand right now that is true, but the situation isn't static. Grayson is only ours for a little while longer and the Coun'hij has got to be recruiting heavily from the dispossessed right now. I've got my feelers out there too, but so far everyone with any real power is holding out for more latitude than I'd be willing to give them. We need to move quickly or the situation could spiral completely out of control. There's never any telling who will manifest a power next and it could just as easily be one of their guys as one of ours."

It was a sobering fact for all that this wasn't the first time that I'd mentioned the possibility. I let them consider what we were up against and then pointed at the files.

"This is everything that Ash, Donovan and I have been able to scrape together about the ghost pack. I want each of you to read through this and then add in anything else you know, have heard or even suspect. I think we need a single point to feed all of this information to. I'd suggest one of you but you each have more on your plate than you're possibly going to be able to get to. Given that, I think we should use Tasha. Vivian would be perfect from the standpoint that she isn't going to be caught up in a big move, but until we've got all of the dominance issues sorted out in the Tonopah pack I think the secret is probably safest with Tasha for now."

Louis was about to offer his opinion when someone started hammering on the door to Donovan's study. Dominic made a beeline to me as soon as the door was open. "Hurry, Alec! Isaac and Wyatt are fighting."

Fighting wasn't quite the right word. I motioned for Jaclyn and the others to follow and then raced along behind Dominic. Less than a minute later Dominic led us around a bend in the garden path and I was finally able to see Isaac and Wyatt. They'd changed to their hybrid forms, but they were convulsing on the ground a dozen feet away from each other.

James and Carson were both bloody and breathing heavily but they were calmly standing next to each other so the only logical explanation was that they'd taken their injuries keeping Isaac and Wyatt away from each other until Grayson arrived.

I was glad that Grayson had made it there before I had. I'd been using my power too frequently as of late, and I continued to worry that one of these times I'd reach for it and it wouldn't respond to my need.

I walked up next to Grayson and gave him a nod. "Can they hear me while you've got them neutralized like this?"

I smiled at Grayson's nod and then stepped between Isaac and Wyatt. "I'm going to guess that this has something to do with Jess, but ultimately it doesn't matter. If you have something to settle then you do it at a time and place of my choosing so that I can make sure you don't kill each other."

Isaac's beast looked up at me with angry eyes and I wished once again that I had a magic solution to the difficulties he and Jess were going through.

"Go ahead and sort out your dominance issues now, but remember that whatever happens here today doesn't do anything to change who's in charge when you're on duty."

I stepped back out of range and then nodded for Grayson to let them up.

The sudden explosion of movement was even more violent than I'd been anticipating. Isaac connected with two long slashes across Wyatt's chest and right arm before dancing back out of range of Wyatt's counterattack.

Isaac's defeat at Abaddon's hands had yielded impressive gains. Isaac had always been a good fighter but he'd gotten faster over the last couple of months. I'd known that Isaac hadn't liked not being able to protect Jess when Agony had visited during the fall, but I hadn't realized that he'd spent quite so much time practicing.

Wyatt charged in with a clear attempt to clinch but Isaac savaged his right arm again and then reversed directions and hit Wyatt hard enough to bowl him over. The impact sent the two of them rolling but Isaac was the first one back up on his feet and he landed another blow to Wyatt's chest before the younger hybrid was able to jump away.

I looked over at James and saw that he'd arrived at the same conclusion that I had. Isaac had been pretty consistently dominant to James for years now, but there was no question any longer. James was going to have to be more careful these days. Isaac was operating on too short of a fuse to put up with James' normal drama and James had very little chance of winning against him now.

Wyatt changed directions with a speed that had been lacking from the first few exchanges and suddenly he had hold of Isaac's right arm with his jaws as his hands tore at Isaac's chest.

The attack lasted only a split second before Isaac broke free, but they were now equally bloody and most of the onlookers seemed to have just realized that Wyatt still had a very real chance of winning.

The next few exchanges were lightning fast. Isaac drove Wyatt before him, claws striking home again and again until suddenly Wyatt made his move, ducking under Isaac's left hand and then sinking his talons into Isaac's leg. I was under no illusions about the completeness of my training, but I'd still never seen anything like this before.

Wyatt grabbed Isaac's arm with his muzzle and straightened out so that Isaac's entire left side was taut as he threw his weight around and took Isaac to the ground. It happened too fast for me to see exactly how Wyatt managed to end up on top, but when the two of them stopped rolling he already had Isaac wrapped up. It wasn't exactly grappling, it wasn't so much joint locks as it was carefully placed claws and talons, but it was obvious that Wyatt had the leverage and he was riding out Isaac's increasingly erratic movements.

It was as inexorable as time. Isaac would thrash about trying to break free while Wyatt waited until the opportune moment and then went for a new hold. Each new hold limited Isaac's options even further until Wyatt was perfectly positioned for a killing strike.

I unleashed my power as soon as it was obvious that Isaac was beaten, dropping both of them into bloody heaps. I pulled Wyatt off of Isaac and towed him over to Carson before turning off my ability.

Wyatt pulled himself back onto two feet and then looked from Isaac over to Jessica, who'd arrived midway through the fight, before letting his form shrink back down.

"I'll see who I want to see and you won't try to tell me otherwise. Not now, not ever."

Chapter 12

Adriana Paige
Graves Estate
Sanctuary, Utah

It felt like my head was going to just fall right off of my shoulders. I was always exhausted these days. It would have been nice if I'd been able to blame it on Alec's ability, but I knew that wasn't the cause.

It was all this stupid wedding stuff. Kami was like a wedding planning superhero, but with Rachel gone there was more for me to do than ever and I absolutely hated all of it. I was picking out cummerbunds and bridesmaid gifts and all of the other things that I'd never expected to have to worry about for years, if ever.

The only saving grace to anything about the planning process was the fact that it was Alec that I was going to be marrying. Actually it wasn't entirely fair to blame my current condition completely on the wedding planning, at least not directly. I was also plenty worried about the fact that my mom had flown into town and was currently less than five minutes away from the estate.

I checked my watch again and then realized that the ETA had been wrong as three vehicles pulled into the massive circular driveway in front of Alec and Rachel's house. I didn't know how they'd managed it around everything else, but James and Ash had been working with some of the world's best bodyguards over the last few weeks and everything they'd been learning had resulted in security arrangements that were even more paranoid than what they'd been able to think of on their own.

Today the 'principal' was in the second vehicle in the convoy but I already knew that Mom was probably going to be in the middle car. They sometimes put us in the first car, but they seemed to prefer the middle SUV and they never put us in the back vehicle.

James escorted my mom into the house while Grayson and the others kept watch. I met Mom at the door and gave her a hug. "Hi, Mom. I hope your flight was okay."

"It was absolutely lovely, dear. I have to say I could really get used to the idea of never flying commercial again. Just bypassing airport security would be more than enough to hook me. When you throw in the gourmet meals it pretty much outclasses everything else."

I found myself smiling. Mom didn't seem to be holding a grudge over the way that Alec and I had pressured her into letting me stay here. I honestly hadn't been sure either way, but this would make the conversation we were about to have much easier than it otherwise would have been.

"I'm glad that Alec was able to spare one of the jets for you. Do you want to swing by your room to freshen up?"

We were passing one of the sitting rooms. I couldn't remember the proper name for it, so I always thought of it as the white leather room. Mom looked over as if she were about to respond and then missed a step.

"Adriana Paige. I raised you from a baby. What secret are you getting ready to ambush me with? You're not pregnant, are you?"

I felt myself blush and looked back at James and Carson who were walking several paces back to give us the faintest illusion of privacy. I knew they'd still be able to hear everything we said, but I couldn't tell my mom that, not without tipping her off to the fact that our bodyguards were more than just human.

"I'm not pregnant, Mom. That would be...well, it would be impossible."

She gave me a look that said she wasn't so sure, but I knew I wasn't pregnant. Alec was holding resolutely to his decision to wait until after we got married. He was right and I agreed with him, but that didn't mean that there weren't occasional times when the temptation made me want to scream.

"Okay, out with it then."

"Can I take you someplace first?"

"How long will it take for us to get there? You know how much I hate not knowing a secret."

"We can be there in fifteen minutes."

Mom gestured for me to lead the way. "Okay, but once we get there just come right out and tell me, no beating around the bush."

The trip out to the park was uneventful despite all of the security. Alec's plan seemed to be working. Jaclyn and Louis' packs hadn't moved yet but they'd started letting shape shifters from south of the border through their territories and it was starting to put more pressure on some of the other packs.

I suspected that some of the people being impacted had already decided that Alec was the devil, but the Flagstaff and Scottsdale packs had just sworn allegiance to him over the last few days. That brought us up to a total strength of six packs, seven if you counted the Chicago pack. It meant that things had gotten even busier around the estate and Alec had continued to increase my traveling security detachment as more bodies had become available.

Mom and I rode in the back of a golf cart this time around. Enough progress had been made on the cobblestone driveway between the house and the park that we didn't have to take the noisy ATV's anymore.

My breath caught a little as we came up over the hill and I saw the park again. I hadn't been out to see it in more than a week and an incredible amount of progress had been made in the intervening time.

The sod had all been put down and the decorative streams were being given their finishing touches. Even more amazing was how gorgeous the decorative arches were looking. Mom grabbed my hand and squeezed it in amazement.

"Adri, is this what you've been working on since you got here? It's breathtaking."

I chuckled despite myself. "If you call spending an obscene amount of Alec's money to hire professionals 'working,' then yes, I've been working on this for weeks now. It's...well, it's going to be where Alec and I get married."

Mom took a deep breath and then mustered up a smile. "I wondered how long it would be before he asked you. I don't see as deeply as Russ does, but even I could see how much he loved you when we were here last. Have you set a date?"

"Yes, but you're not going to be happy...it's really, really soon."

"How come I'm not surprised?"

"Maybe because you're used to your daughter doing stupid things?"

She frowned at that. "Do you think marrying Alec is stupid?"

"No. I don't think marrying Alec is stupid, I don't even think that marrying Alec this quickly is stupid. I do think it's stupid to try and put together such a massive ceremony this quickly though."

I got another of those knowing mother looks and then she looked back out over the park and nodded. "It's gorgeous, but you're right, this isn't you, Adri, not really. Have you told Alec?"

I shook my head. "He's got a lot on his mind right now. Besides, he warned me in advance that our wedding would be completely over the top."

"You may be right that nothing can be done about the situation, Adri, but you owe it to Alec to at least tell him what you're feeling. If you're not careful the two of you will grow apart without even realizing it's happening."

"Okay, you're probably right, Mom. I'll talk to Alec and tell him that the lavish amounts of money he's spending on the wedding aren't my cup of tea."

She shook her head at my half joke and then sighed and leaned in close enough she could whisper. "Is Alec involved in something illegal, dear?"

It was the absolute last thing I'd expected out of my mom, but I managed to keep my voice level as I responded.

"Why would you even ask that?"

"I'm fairly oblivious to most things, sweetie, but even I can tell that all of these buff young men are bodyguards. The group that picked us up from the airport last time wasn't nearly this big. What's happened?"

"Alec pissed off some really powerful people by doing the right thing a little while ago. It's just a precaution really, but it makes him happy to know that I'm safe. Alec isn't into anything he shouldn't be, trust me on that one."

I got another considering look and then she finally nodded her acceptance of my answer. "Are you happy, sweetie? Are you really sure that this is what *you* want to do? Not something that you feel like you should be doing, but really something that you want with all of your heart?"

That question was easier to answer. "Yes, Mom. I'm not keen on how swanky the wedding is going to be and I don't love having a bodyguard within shouting distance twenty-four hours a day, but I love Alec and I want to marry him more than anything else."

"Okay. I won't get in the way then. I'll sign whatever papers you need me to sign since you're a minor, but only on one condition."

My chest tightened up but I took a deep breath to steel myself against whatever it was and then nodded. I almost fell out of the cart when she pulled an engagement ring out of her pocket and slid it onto her finger.

"Russ asked me to marry him. Our ceremony won't be for months still, but I want you there when it takes place."

I felt tears making their way down my face. It was so soon after Dad had died, but somehow that wasn't as important anymore. I was gone, which meant that Mom was all alone. If Russ made her happy then I wasn't going to stand in her way. Besides, despite my best efforts Russ had grown on me.

"Of course I'll be there, Mom. Wild horses couldn't keep me away."

We spent nearly an hour walking through the park. I showed her all of the little bells and whistles that Rachel and Kami had added to the area. The conversation was less strained than I remembered it being from before. Even more amazingly, Mom talked less about work than she used to. Instead she told me about dates with Russ, romantic dinners and fun day trips that they'd taken over the last few weeks.

Once I got over my amazement that anything had managed to tear Mom away from work, I found myself smiling more than I had in a long time. If Russ had been able to remind my mom that there was more to life than photography then he really was the right guy for her.

We'd just finished looking at the hedges around the lip of the amphitheater when Carson and James hurried over.

"We need to get back to the mansion right now."

I didn't resist as Carson grabbed my arm and guided me back to the cart. "What happened?"

"The main power feed to the house from the city just went down but the houses in Sanctuary still have power."

"So the first move in some kind of attack?"

"It's hard to say. The backup generator kicked on without any problems so there hasn't been any kind of breach in our security yet, but we should get you both back to the house now just in case."

Instead of getting in the cart Carson led me over to one of the ATV's that were parked nearby and then brought his hand up so that he could talk into his radio.

"Snowflake is returning from the oasis. Support would be appreciated."

A few seconds later we were tearing cross-country back towards the house. The ride was the kind of hair-raising trip that you could only manage with superhuman reflexes, but it made sense that Carson wouldn't want to bring me back via the normal route.

I risked a look back to verify that James and Mom weren't too far back and nearly lost my grip on Carson when he took us around a particularly tight corner. After that I paid more attention to where we were going. Halfway to the estate Isaac and Dominic came into view driving matched ATVs and I caught a flicker of movement out of the corner of my eye that I was pretty sure was Peter and Jane shadowing us on four legs.

Mom had probably forgotten that we'd started out with four bodyguards, but I hadn't. Knowing that the two wolves from the Tucson pack were out there using their superior noses to make sure that we weren't ambushed was an even greater reassurance than I'd expected it to be.

Less than five minutes after the alarm sounded, Mom and I were being ushered into the house. Mom was taking the whole thing more calmly than I'd expected her to, but I knew I was going to have to answer some difficult questions once she was convinced that we were safe again. I was busy trying to come up with reassurances that weren't outright lies when the lights suddenly went out.

There was enough light from nearby windows to prevent total darkness, but Mom grabbed my hand with fear-born strength at a second sign that we were probably under attack. I gasped in pain and collapsed into the wall. As Carson started to pull me back to my feet I realized that I could hear someone through the wall.

"...no, I haven't changed my mind. I'm not going to go talk to her, but that doesn't mean that you shouldn't still be keeping tabs on her. Then find her, damn it! She's more important than you know. If I don't *know* that she's okay then it's going to be that much harder to stop myself from going to her. No, you don't have any idea what the fallout would be like if that happened."

The power went back on, drowning the voice out in a storm of white noise as Carson finally lost patience with me and bodily picked me up. The trip down to the secure vault under the mansion took another five minutes, but I spent every second of it wondering who Shawn had been talking to.

Chapter 13

Alec Graves
Graves Estate
Sanctuary, Utah

I hadn't spent nearly enough time with Adri lately, but the craziness of our second phantom alarm nearly caused me to put off our date for a second time. Our loss of power hadn't ended up being an attack, but it had still been concerning. If it had been any other day I might have let circumstances get in the way, but I couldn't do that, not for this particular date.

It wasn't supposed to be possible for the entire house to lose power like that. Donovan and I had rushed down to the backup generator only moments after the lights had gone out. I'd been expecting sabotage. I hadn't expected for it to be Rachel.

She'd given me a cheery smile and then looked up at the ceiling for several seconds before absently restarting the generator and then skipping over to me without a word. Once we were back in her room I tried for several seconds to get an answer out of her as to why she'd killed the power, but she'd just pointed out the window she'd used to escape her room and mumbled something about a storm.

Dominic had been mortified that Rachel had slipped away during Dom's shift, but none of us had expected Rachel to sneak out like that. It was one more thing to worry about, but at least Vivian's return and her willingness to swear fealty meant that we had enough females in the house to keep a constant watch on Rachel now without using Jess, who was less and less reliable with each day that passed.

Once Rachel was safely tucked away again, I'd then had to spend nearly two hours reassuring various guests that it all hadn't been some kind of attack by the Coun'hij. That in turn made me late for dinner with Adri and her mom which proved to be a pleasant, if occasionally tense, affair.

Dinner ran long, partly because I wanted to spend extra time with my future mother-in-law, and partly because I just couldn't bear to tear myself away from Adri once I was actually with her. Once I did finally excuse myself from the table, I stole two hours with Donovan to review finances and then I crammed in a session lifting weights on the machine.

The next day arrived too soon. I only needed a few hours of sleep each night, but I still felt like I'd come up half an hour short. Given all of the other demands on my time, the last thing I wanted to be doing was to spend an hour running, but I wasn't a human-style CEO. My ability was currently providing me a pass when it came to physical confrontations, but I knew it would be foolish to let my conditioning slide. My ability probably wouldn't work on a werewolf, and even if it did, it was only a matter of time before I ran into some other situation that could only be dealt with using claws and talons.

Jasmin and Dominic accompanied me on my run since they were the only two who could keep up with me. We shifted to four legs and ran along an arc that toured the very edge of our territory. Despite my begrudging the time involved, there was no arguing with the fact that I enjoyed the act of running.

Being in the dark, on four legs, with the soft light of trees and bushes flickering past me, was an almost Zen-like experience. Taking a motorcycle or a car right up to its limits came close, but still didn't touch this. There was nothing between my paws and the ground and I relished the instant feedback as I threw myself over fallen trees and around large rocks.

By the end of the run, Jasmin and I were panting and all three of us were exhausted. Dominic fell into formation on my left side as we entered the garden and I suddenly realized that she'd put on another inch through the shoulder. I found myself smiling inside as I realized that someone was going to get a surprise today during our sparring session. If Dom was putting on a growth spurt then she was going to be correspondingly stronger and faster.

By the time I'd had breakfast, sat through the longest formal reception yet, and then had lunch, I was more than ready for the sparring session that followed. Unfortunately the sparring session wasn't as satisfying as I'd expected it to be. Shawn's presence at the estate, but not his purpose, had leaked, so he joined us and then I proceeded to run him all around the circle of sand.

I'd expected as much given that Shawn hadn't spent the last few years in a state of near-constant skirmish with Brandon's pack like I had, but I didn't expect for Grayson to do much the same to me.

At first I thought I was just losing my edge, but that wasn't it. I hit Grayson with some of my best moves and he countered them with combinations that I'd never seen. He was aggressive, but there was something missing there, maybe a lack of commitment that would have otherwise allowed him to take me down in the first few seconds of the fight. As it was I managed to stretch things out for nearly a full minute before he finally managed a clinch and took me to the ground.

He demonstrated greater than usual control of his beast and rolled away without having to be pulled off of me, but even after he was several feet away I stayed on the ground reconstructing the last few seconds of the fight. It was like the difference between a street fighter and a classically trained martial artist. I had experience and pure aggression on my side, but he'd stayed a step ahead of me nearly the entire fight. It could have gone the other way with a little luck on my side, but it was one more piece of evidence that there was more to Grayson than met the eye. No dispossessed would have such a complete breadth of training. There were only a few packs that had maintained their integrity for long enough to be able to muster the knowledge base required to produce someone like Grayson.

Ulrich's pack topped the list, but I knew Grayson hadn't ever belonged to the Chicago pack, just like I knew he hadn't been part of any of the others that were possibilities. He was still holding out on me and I was running out of time to convince him that I was one of the good guys.

For all that I'd received the most thorough trouncing I'd suffered through in months, the sparring session was over all too soon. I cleaned up and then jumped on an encrypted conference call with Ash, Donovan, and the pack leaders who'd sworn to me. Just because they'd promised obedience didn't mean that they were all completely ready to give up jockeying for position, and I nearly lost my temper more than once during the course of the call. The only thing that got me through the call was the knowledge that Adri would be waiting for me as soon as we were done.

Once the call was done, I confirmed with Donovan that the arrangements for our date were all completed and then went looking for Adri. I found her waiting for me in my room with a copy of *Pride and Prejudice* resting open on her lap.

"Happy Valentine's Day, Adri."

I leaned in and kissed her and then realized as I drew back just how tired she looked.

"Are you okay, Adri?"

"Yeah, I'm fine. Having Mom here just took more out of me than I expected it to. Did you know that Russ proposed?"

I double-checked that my ability wasn't subconsciously draining her and then shook my head in response to her question. "I didn't know—I don't keep a really close eye on her, but I can start doing so if you want me to."

"No, it's okay. I suspect that Russ is more than capable of doing that all by himself. What do you think of the idea of them getting married?"

I shrugged. "She's not my mom, Adri. What really matters is how you feel about it."

"I guess you're right. I'm happy for her, it just feels really, really odd for her to be marrying again already."

I gently picked the book up off of her knees and set it on the table beside her before pulling her to her feet.

"For whatever it's worth I didn't turn up any kind of dirt on Russ in any of the checks we did on him. I think he's a very capable, very good guy. Your mom could do a lot worse."

She leaned into me and wrapped her arms around my shoulders. "Russ sounds an awful lot like someone else I know."

The trip out to the far greenhouse took nearly twenty minutes, but it was all worth it when I got to see the expression on Adri's face as I led her into our own little tropical paradise. Nearly every kind of fruit could be found somewhere inside this particular greenhouse and Adri seemed eager to go explore.

I laughed and then nudged her towards the raspberries. "They are through that door on the right side. Here's a basket, you go ahead. I'll put out the blanket and then join you in a minute."

The picnic basket was perfect. With all of the new arrivals we'd had to hire a cook and Donovan had made sure that she'd included plenty of warm, fresh-baked bread and enough butter to slather every piece in yellow goodness and still have half the tin left over. I spread everything out and then picked up an empty container and followed Adri's scent trail. She'd covered the bottom of her bucket with raspberries and then moved on through the various separate sections of the greenhouse collecting tangerines, guava fruit and kiwis. She seemed to be debating over a casaba melon when I finally caught up to her.

When she wasn't looking I carefully set a grapefruit, which I knew she hated, into her basket and then lifted her up so that she could reach the bottom of an unusually tall peach tree. Our conversation was relaxed and natural for the next twenty minutes while we filled our respective buckets up with fruit.

Back at the blanket we slowly worked our way through a combination of what Donovan had sent along and the stuff that we'd gathered from inside the greenhouse. Adri cocked her head to the side when I started in on my second loaf of bread. "I thought I was the bread lover."

"You are, I'm just trying to make sure that I consume enough calories that I'm not hungry sometime in the next two hours."

She nodded and popped a raspberry into her mouth. "This was perfect, Alec. It reminds me of when we were first together. Simple activities that didn't get in the way of you and I getting to know each other."

I found myself smiling. "Just wait until you have to mix your own dessert. You'll start singing a different tune then."

Adri grabbed a container of vanilla yogurt and mixed pieces of tangerine into it. "Nope, I'm still happy. I know that my life is going to be pretty high-profile in some ways after marrying you, but it's memories like this that will keep me going through all of that."

I used my spoon to sample a bit of her yogurt and gave her a nod. "You should market that stuff, it's really quite good. I think it needs more grapefruit though."

Adri stuck her tongue out at me and we both laughed for a couple of minutes. Once the laughter died down I reached over and tucked a stray strand of hair behind her left ear. "This has been hard on you, hasn't it?"

"Honestly? Yes. Not just all the craziness of the wedding prep, although that has been plenty odious. It's all of the other girls too."

"Adri, you know I'd never..."

She interrupted me with a quick headshake. "I know you're not responding to any of their advances, but it's still hard to see them throwing themselves at you again and again. It's...well, it's like I get daily evidence that if you ever got the least bit tired of me that you'd have plenty of other options."

She looked away from me for several seconds and sighed. "I've been wanting to talk to you about how much I hate planning for the wedding, but I haven't. Partly because you warned me that it was going to be like this back when you proposed, but mostly it's because I don't want to seem ungrateful, don't want to make you second-guess your decision to marry me in the first place. Mom told me that I should talk to you about it though."

I pulled her back around so that I could see her face and then I kissed her forehead. "Adri, I wish you would have said something sooner. Your mom was right, you should always bring these kinds of concerns to me. Do you really think the fact that you prefer not to spend money would make me second-guess marrying you? Half of those girls who are throwing themselves at me would make one exorbitant demand after another if they were in your shoes, just to see what they could get away with."

She looked up at me with the barest glimmer of hope in her expression and I smiled at her. "I think you're amazing on every level. I'm doing what I can to keep our guests in check, but if it will make you happy I'll send them all home and we can have the simple ceremony that you want."

The offer hung in the air between us for several seconds before she shook her head again. "No, I knew what I was getting into and besides, it would be the wrong answer. You need to handle the other packs however you think gives us the best chance of recruiting them to our side. Everything depends on that. Not just my happiness but the survival of everyone who depends on you. I haven't forgotten what Shawn told us and I haven't forgotten that I swore to do everything in my power to support you in your quest to take down the Coun'hij and see your people free once again."

"Not my people, our people. We are off to a small start but things are starting to come together. They'll start to snowball from here and before you know it we'll be safe, truly safe, again."

"Our people?"

"Yes, our people. I couldn't do all of this without you."

Adri pulled me down into a kiss and for a while nothing else mattered.

Chapter 14

Dominic Sanchez
Abandoned Industrial Park
Cedar City, Utah

It was nice to be spending a night away from the house, but I couldn't help but feel guilty at the same time. Rachel was doing worse than ever and there wasn't anything I could do but sit there and watch. I'd tried to exercise my supposed healing talent, but nothing had happened. For a second or two I'd almost felt like I was touching something bigger than just Rachel or me, but then it disappeared and I was left with the same result as the time I'd tried to heal James. In a word, nothing.

The patrols that Alec had started having people run weren't necessarily the kind of thing that most people wanted to be doing, but it was better than sitting there and watching Rachel talk to people who weren't in the room with us. Sometimes she didn't even seem to be able to hear me when I tried to talk to her.

Jess reached for the stereo and it was all I could do not to hiss at her. We were the wheels for this particular excursion. That meant that we were supposed to be listening to the handheld radio, not rocking out to whatever new song Wyatt had introduced Jess to.

I told myself to calm down as I took a right turn so that we'd be able to continue to shadow James and Peter. I didn't particularly like Jess' current choice in crushes, but at least some of that was because I knew exactly how much she and Isaac had been through before Oblivion had stolen her memories. *She* didn't remember that, not any more at least, so I needed to cut her a break, at least a little bit of one.

It would have been easier if she wasn't behaving stupidly in so many other respects. This wasn't a punishment detail for the rest of us, but it definitely was for Jess. Since she'd left Rachel on her own Alec had kept her busy with one mission after another, but she still found time to hang out with Wyatt somehow.

Alec was pretty shrewd, but I was starting to think that he was getting too clever this time around. The patrol needed to be run—we couldn't let the disappearance of five people in two days go uninvestigated this close to our territory—but she didn't need to be here. Rather than punishing her, he was actually just punishing the rest of us with her presence.

The two-way radio crackled with static and then James' voice reached out of it and soothed away some of my irritation. "Our nose thinks that he's found the scent of one of our missing people. He's headed north."

I grabbed the transmitter before Jess could pick it up and say something that would piss James off. "Werewolves don't usually drag their victims this far out to kill them."

"Yeah, I know. They also don't usually leave them alive for this long. I'm starting to think that we're dealing with something else."

"Not bloodsuckers?"

"Nope, the whole town smells wonderfully vampire-free. No, best bet is just some psycho dayborn."

We'd borrowed the setup for these patrols from the Tucson pack. They had a long history of hunting werewolves despite the Coun'hij's orders not to do so, and Peter was their go-to guy for this kind of thing. Peter had been ranging around on four legs for the last two hours as our 'nose' with James following along behind in his normal shape so that he could provide backup if Peter got jumped.

Jess and I were supposed to stay close enough for the guys to be able to use us as a getaway car but not so close that we'd get pulled into a trap ourselves.

The silence after James' last transmission lasted only a few seconds before Jess used her bubblegum to blow a massive bubble. "You're lucky to have James. He doesn't seem nearly as annoying as Isaac."

I shook my head. "James and I have our share of problems, but we work at it and so far things have worked out. Having a relationship is never easy."

I must have let a little more of my frustration slip into my voice than I'd realized. Jess sat in silence for several seconds before trying again. "So are you going to swear one of these stupid oaths to Alec?"

"Yes, I am. I would have done so already but James asked me to wait a few weeks so he could think things over."

"Why? I know you guys think Alec hung the moon, but all he's done lately is order people around and spend a lot of time behind closed doors."

"That's kind of a personal thing to be asking me. Besides, I'm not sure you'd understand even if I tried to explain it."

"I'm sorry if I'm prying. I guess I just don't understand why anyone would voluntarily give up their freedom like that."

Jess suddenly looked very much like she had just after Oblivion had stolen her memories. She was like a lost child who wasn't quite sure where the world she knew had gone. Maybe her usual flightiness was just an attempt to cover up the fact that she still didn't feel like she had a place with us. I needed to give her the benefit of the doubt.

"Alec saved my life. You all did, but him most of all. None of the rest of you would have stood up to my father like that if Alec hadn't ordered you to help me. It's more than that though. I spent most of my life in a place where might was the only law. It's not the kind of place anyone should ever have to live in."

Jess looked over at me with confusion on her face but she waited for me to find the words I needed to go on.

"People sometimes think that what you all live in here is the normal state of things, but it isn't. Civilization is an aberration. It's the best arrangement, but it only takes place when the strongest, the most dangerous among us choose to put aside their self-interest and create a new order, one where the weak are protected. That is what Alec represents. The Coun'hij is nothing more than a bunch of thugs who meddle less than they could, but who ultimately are just in it for themselves."

"You think that Alec will create a new era for our people."

"I don't know. Nearly everything imaginable is arrayed against him, but I hope so. I hope that he'll create a new era for your people and then that he'll turn his eyes south and save my people too."

"Is that even possible?"

"I don't know. You remember how deadly Anton was? There will be dozens, maybe hundreds more like him in South America, each of them living like a tiny despot and completely unwilling to see a new order put into place."

I seemed to have finally gotten through to Jess and she sat in silence for several seconds as she considered what I'd told her. "Do you think that we'd be able to recruit some of your people to our side?"

"I don't know. I never met anyone down there that I really trusted, at least not anyone who is still alive, but Alec is considering the possibility already. He asked me the other day if I knew anyone from back home who might be sympathetic to our cause. I think he would really like to recruit someone who can track like Anton could, but Alec didn't get into any specifics beyond that."

Whatever Jess would have said was cut off by James' voice coming through the radio. "Girls, I need you both out here right now. The nose thinks he's found all five of the missing people but we're not going in there by ourselves."

Five minutes later Jess and I were standing outside the door to a massive old building as James and Peter finished circling the building to make sure that the missing people hadn't left out another door.

James took a deep breath and then pointed at the door. "Okay, it's not vampires and it doesn't feel like werewolves but that doesn't mean that whoever kidnapped these people isn't dangerous so we go in together, Peter in the front, then me, with Dom bringing up the rear. Keep your eyes open and don't forget the rest of your senses."

Jess and I both nodded and then stripped down to our ha'bits and changed into four legs with a ripple of power. James tested the door and found it locked but his claws punched right through the sheet metal and once he had a decent-sized hole it was a simple matter to reach through and unbar the door.

Peter ghosted into the darkness without any hesitation, which spoke volumes to the amount of trust he had in James specifically and the rest of us generally. Nobody liked being point in a dangerous situation, but he was the best choice given just how sensitive his nose was.

A low whine made its way back to us as Jess entered the building, but I didn't understand what was bothering Peter until I was several feet in myself. The entire building had been sprayed with a combination of vinegar and something else that burned my nose with surprising intensity.

It was a bad sign, but James seemed determined to investigate and I didn't have a good way of speaking out in this form, even assuming that I wanted to get into an argument with him in the middle of an operation.

It almost seemed like we were in an old slaughterhouse. There was a maze of steel panels crisscrossing the open space that looked like they would be overkill for containing cows. I couldn't smell anything over the vinegar but Peter seemed to be getting a whiff of something that was leading him deeper and deeper into the building.

It smelled like a trap and I didn't like all of the dead metal, but other than the four of us there wasn't anything else showing the glow of a living organism. I could tell that James was getting jittery too, but Peter was single-mindedly moving deeper into the darkness.

James took a step forward to call Peter back to us, Jess tight against his flank, when it happened. Massive sheets of steel dropped down from above locking the three of them inside the maze of stock panels. James might have made it out but Jess was too close and she didn't react quickly enough.

James hit the barrier with his shoulder, but although he managed to shake the massive improvised cage nothing gave way. I heard Peter moving forward, cautiously looking for a way out, but I had other worries.

A dimly glowing figure had just stepped out from behind a screen of some kind and he was approaching me slowly with a sword gripped loosely in one hand. He stopped well outside of striking range, fiddled momentarily with something in his hand and then the lights inside the building came on.

I blinked away spots as I backed up to put more space between us, but he didn't move forward to capitalize on his advantage and as my vision started to clear I noticed just how familiar my opponent looked.

He was a middle-aged Asian man with a nondescript build, but it was the eyes that finally made things click into place for me. I'd seen those cold eyes once before when I was little more than a child after days of being stalked by a myth that I'd been so sure didn't really exist.

The Hunter had found me a second time.

I heard James yelling for me to get them out, but the opponent between them and me was one I knew I couldn't beat. The Hunter took a few steps forward, his sword gleaming darkly in his hand, and then threw a packet of papers at my feet.

"Vanessa sends her regards. You're going to want to give everything else in there to your alpha. He's going to need to take care of a couple of problems or they'll come back to bite him in unexpected ways."

Old terror tried to overwhelm me, but my beast provided me with surprising strength and instead of retreating further I found myself slowly advancing. The Hunter smiled slightly like an adult who was amused at the antics of a child and then brought his weapon up into a guard position.

"You've done well for yourself since I last saw you. You've vindicated my decision to allow *his* grand experiment to proceed, but never forget that I'm watching from the shadows. *He's* been wrong before."

A slight movement of his fingers was the only warning I got. One second the entire building was bathed in light, the next harsh strobes flashed with blinding intensity.

I heard the Hunter turn and walk away but was in too much pain to try and follow him, especially considering that I'd be stumbling around blind. Fifteen minutes later, after the spots had cleared from my vision, I changed back to my two-legged form and picked up the packet of papers from the ground where The Hunter had thrown them.

The envelope on the top was addressed to me in a flowing script that matched the autograph on the books back in my room at the manor. Unsure why I was doing so, I slipped the envelope inside of my ha'bit before walking over to the steel panels and finding a way to release James and the others.

James didn't calm down until they were released. He'd been throwing himself at the panels the entire time I'd been disabled, and I knew without looking that he was going to have bruises all over his upper body.

"Who was that, Dom?"

I almost laughed at James' question, but I managed to keep my composure. It wasn't just that James would have felt insulted if I'd laughed. I was pretty sure that the laughter would come out with all of the hysteria that I was feeling inside and I couldn't risk that. Alec was going to need to believe me when I told my story to him. I didn't know very much about Vanessa still, but any warning that she'd sent me would be important. We couldn't afford to have Alec dismiss it.

"He's a ghost, James. When I was growing up there were legends of a hunter who tracked down my kind and killed them. The only thing that the legends agreed on was that nobody had ever survived for long once he found them."

"So he's found you now?"

"No, he found me years ago, before I ever left home. I don't know why he spared me then any more than I know why he spared me now."

The answer didn't fully satisfy James but he knew me well enough to know that I'd tell him whatever I could once we were alone together. The trip back was pure torture. I didn't get a chance to read my letter until we'd made it back to the manor and I snuck off to the bathroom.

I'm sorry I can't tell you more, Dominic. You really are a healer and more than you know is going to depend on you being able to use your ability. You're on the right track, but don't waste

your time on Rachel, she can't be helped at this
point.

Do whatever it takes to convince Alec to
investigate the two locations in the packet. One of
those cats is a tracker. If Alec can't defeat these
adversaries then all is lost.

I won't be able to help much more after this.
The future is becoming too clouded for me to
commit some of the atrocities I'm being told need
to take place.

Chapter 15

Isaac Nazir
City Limits
Las Vegas, Nevada

Jess had been avoiding me ever since my fight with Wyatt, but I still could have managed to spend some time with her if Alec hadn't been running me so hard. We had more muscle around the house these days than we'd had even a couple of weeks before, but there was still more to do than we had time for.

The wedding was just around the corner too, which would make things even worse. I'd spent most of the last week ferrying VIPs back and forth to the airport. Once the wedding guests started arriving things would just get even more hectic.

Alec was typically elusive. Those who had sworn an oath of fealty to him seemed to get a few minutes here and there, but the rest of us might as well not have existed. I got my orders every day from Ash of all people, but the one and only time I'd tried to push back and assert my dominance, Grayson had intervened and told me to go do my job before he was forced to drop me.

I knew why Alec was doing what he was doing, but it didn't make it any easier to deal with. We'd been through years of hell together already. I shouldn't have to swear an oath to him to still be in his inner circle, not even after some of our recent difficulties.

This particular mission was just more salt in the wound. Dominic had come back from her last outing with a map and a cryptic warning from some guy with a sword. I would have sent two or three guys to case out the area, but Alec had chosen to mount the equivalent of a full-scale invasion.

Alec had stayed behind with James and Jess, but he'd sent most of Jaclyn's pack because he figured that they had the most experience hunting both the cats and the werewolves. Jasmin, Dom and I were along for the ride as well as a big bruiser from Tonopah named Rex. I would have figured that for plenty of firepower for anything we were likely to run into, but Alec had included the terrible trio of Grayson, Wyatt and Carson too.

I figured that meant that most of us would just sit around. If Jaclyn and Grayson couldn't deal with whatever we were running into then we were probably screwed regardless.

The only other thing that had taken me by surprise was the fact that Alec had sent along a dozen cages in a tractor-pulled trailer that we'd had to wait an extra hour for. Hopefully he wasn't too serious about us trying to capture whatever was out here.

Jaclyn looked around the hotel conference room that we were using as a base of operations and then waved everyone in so that they could see the map she'd laid out.

"Okay, Peter and Arnold just finished running a quick circuit around our target area. No sign of vampires which tends to bear out Dominic's intel. We think that we're up against a bunch of cats but I don't want anyone to be too surprised if it turns out that we've got a different threat on our hands."

There was a low rumble as people digested the news, but it was obvious that a few key people had already known. Predictably, it was the 'oathers' as I was starting to think of them, who had received an advance briefing of what we were likely to be up against.

Jaclyn continued before the speculation could get out of hand. "Based on the density and locations of the scent trails going into the complex, Peter is pretty sure that our guys and gals are in the northeast building. The best-case scenario is that we keep them bottled up inside the building. If they get out in the open we're going to have a tough time catching them, so I'm opting for a layered deployment."

The map already had four dots on it in a loose cordon around the building in question, but Jaclyn went ahead and pointed them out as she named off the team leaders for each location.

"Rex, Brutus, Alexei and Wyatt will each have a couple of wolves under their command. Dominic will be on the north team with Alexei. You wolves will be responsible for intercepting any runners, but remember that if we are up against cats that they'll probably be faster and stronger than you, so don't be heroes. Slow them down, lock them up just long enough for the rest of your team to get there and help you. Depending on how bad things are inside the building, we'll try to send someone after anyone that leaves the building so that you'll have a heavy numerical advantage."

Carson made some kind of gesture at Wyatt, but Jaclyn was talking again so I focused back on her.

"Grayson and I will each take a team into the building from here and here and try to neutralize everyone in the building. If we're up against cats like we think we are then we're going to try and capture as many of them as we can. Focus on anyone that Grayson hasn't incapacitated first. Once we're confident that we've subdued everyone and there aren't any runners then the four teams on the outside of the building will bring the cages in."

Rex held up a hand. "What if it's not a bunch of cats that we're up against?"

"If it's vampires or werewolves then we kill them all, as quickly as we can. Honestly, the worst-case scenario is pretty much that we're up against a large den of werewolves. If that happens then the interior teams will be fighting a delaying action while we wait for the perimeter teams to collapse in and help."

Jaclyn looked around the gathered moonborn and nodded at what she saw in our faces. "Does anyone have any questions before I release you to huddle up with your team leaders?"

Wyatt nodded even before she finished speaking. "Yeah, I've got a question. You told me I was a team leader, but you didn't say anything about sitting this one out on the sidelines. I want in on one of the two inside teams."

Whatever Jaclyn might have said was cut off by Carson's response. "You've got your orders and you're sworn to obey Alec, which means by extension you're sworn to obey Jaclyn when she speaks for him. Shut up and soldier."

"No. Don't think I don't know that this is your doing. I want in on the action."

Grayson's expression was cold enough to freeze water. "You're forgetting your place, Wyatt. Jaclyn is dominant to you in every sense of the word. If you keep pushing she can defeat you like the child you are, but if she chooses not to exercise that right then I'll do it for her and then I'll send you home in dishonor."

It seemed like a pretty weak threat to me, but it shut Wyatt up instantly. He still wasn't happy about his role, but I could tell that he wasn't going to argue anymore. There was something there that I still didn't understand. It should be clear who was in charge of the terrible trio, but I could never tell from what day to the next who was going to step up and speak for the three of them. Today it seemed to be Carson, but Grayson had backed his play without blinking, which went against almost every instinct inherent to our kind.

Apparently satisfied that Grayson and Carson had Wyatt in hand, Jaclyn dismissed us with a wave. The team leaders started calling out names. I waited for several seconds for someone to call for me, but then looked up and found Grayson standing in front of me.

"You're with me, Nazir. Over this way."

Our team consisted of Grayson, and Carson from the terrible trio, Arnold from the Tucson pack, Jasmin, and me. Jaclyn's team was larger, presumably because her ability wasn't able to drop a dozen opponents at a time like Grayson's could.

Once we were all over in one corner of the conference room, Grayson started briefing Arnold and Jasmin while Carson turned to me.

"Assuming that we're not up against werewolves, you and I will have the job of protecting Grayson while the other two deal with anything else we run up against. While he's immobilizing someone he's vulnerable himself."

"Why me instead of Arnold?"

Carson shrugged. "It was Grayson's call. It's his skin so he's the one who gets to pick his bodyguards."

"He'd have been better off with Wyatt. After all, I was the one who lost that match."

Carson shook his head and then led me out of the room where we wouldn't be so easily overheard. "No. Wyatt is pretty sharp, but he's still just a kid. He's never done this, not for real, and a couple of fancy grappling tricks that work in one-on-one fights aren't much use against any of the stuff that we're likely to run into tonight."

"I'm not much older than Wyatt."

"It's true, but you've done this before. You helped bag those four werewolves with the Tucson pack, you guys took down a group of vampires just a few months ago, and after that you got stuck in against that cat that was after Ash and his girl. You're the real deal."

I felt a flash of surprise. I hadn't realized that Carson and his buddies were so well-informed. "I...thanks. I appreciate the vote of confidence."

"It's no more than you deserve. If you want, once we're back at the estate, I can teach you counters to some of the moves Wyatt used on you the other day."

"Why would you do that?"

I got another lazy shrug, but when it became obvious that I wasn't going to let him get away with that, Carson sighed.

"It's obvious that Jess isn't yours, and you're not helping your cause by treating her like a piece of property, but Wyatt shouldn't be sticking his nose in the middle of all of that. He's...well, he's got commitments that aren't being well served by getting involved with anyone here."

Getting to the building where we thought the cats were located turned out to be every bit as much of a madhouse as I'd expected, but forty-five minutes after the briefing concluded we were all onsite and ready to go.

We were waiting just around the corner of the block, safely out of sight from the building, when Jaclyn sent the signal to proceed. I'd had my doubt about the wisdom of splitting the various packs up like she had, but at least on our end everyone swung into action without a hitch.

Arnold and Jasmin raced forward on four legs with the other three of us in hot pursuit. As we reached the building, Carson transformed into his hybrid form and ripped our door right off of its hinges. Jasmin and Arnold ducked into the building and I hurried in after them.

I felt a many-pointed rush of power as Arnold, Grayson and I shifted into our hybrid forms now that we were safely hidden inside the building. Carson took up the tail position, putting himself between Grayson and any attack like he'd done all of this many times before.

We were navigating a series of dark halls right now, but the blueprints that Jaclyn's contacts had provided us indicated that we'd be getting to the large, open center any second.

I followed Arnold around a bend in the hall and then I was in the middle of what felt like the end of the world. Nearly a dozen feline forms streaked through the darkness. They started moving away from us until Jaclyn and her larger group stepped out of a hallway on the far end of the building.

All twelve cats stuttered to a stop for just a split second and then they turned and headed back our way. The fight was on and Jaclyn's plan hadn't survived contact with the enemy any more than I'd expected it to. Grayson stepped out from behind me and cut loose with his power. I felt the fringes of what he hit them with and I was incredibly grateful that he was on our side as six of the cats went down in writhing, hissing heaps.

Carson swore and pushed his way past Grayson. "The six that are left are going to be the most dangerous."

A split second before the unaffected cats hit us, Grayson redirected his power. It was spectacular, but it almost wasn't enough. This batch really was the more dangerous, that or maybe Grayson was just tired from temporarily dropping the first six. Whatever the reason, Grayson only managed to affect three of the ones closest to us.

Jaclyn's people caught up with the first six, who were back on their feet and predictably unhappy, and then the three most dangerous cats hit us. I caught a glimpse of Arnold and Jasmin engaging one, heard Carson tackle another, and then it was my turn.

My guy was fast, nearly as fast as Anton had been when we'd fought him with Alec's power slowing him slightly. I saw him set his back legs and knew that I wasn't going to be able to keep up with him so I guessed that he was going to make a try for Grayson.

I threw myself forward and to the right and managed to get some claws into the cat's side as he sailed by impossibly fast. He hit the ground a few feet short of Grayson and then spun around, tearing furiously at my arm. He was right, I wasn't a match for him, but I didn't need to beat him, I just needed to wrap him up for long enough that Jaclyn and the others could make it over and take him off of my hands.

I closed my fist with my claws still inside of him and spun him around as I picked him up and threw him into a piece of heavy machinery. I had the leverage, but he was still stronger and faster than me. In the last second before he hit, he twisted around violently. It was nearly enough for him to tear free of my grasp, but although it failed to free him, it did manage to turn him enough that he took the impact on his legs.

He still hit hard enough that he would have had broken legs if he'd been a wolf, but he jumped away with my hand still lodged in his side as I heard steps running my direction. I tried to spin him back around so that I could see who was approaching us, but he dug all four legs in and jerked me towards him, pulling me off balance.

It was one of those key decision points in a fight. I needed to let go and make sure that I wasn't about to be ambushed, but if I did that then he'd attack Grayson. If Grayson was forced to let the three he was neutralizing go and they were as bad as this guy then we were going to lose people.

Instead of letting go I dropped to my knees as I whipped my left arm around so that it was between the footsteps behind me and my neck. It was a one in a million effort but it worked. I felt two-hundred and seventy pounds of jaguar get tangled up in my claws and then I was on the ground with two angry cats tearing at me.

I tried to use my talons to keep them away but I wasn't having much luck. The only thing that was saving me was the fact that I had hold of each of them. My grip started to slip on the first shape shifter, but I forced my hand closed with every ounce of will I possessed even as I felt his claws work their way up my arm.

He was inches from opening up the massive arteries along my throat when he started to convulse slightly. It wasn't the full Grayson treatment, but it was enough for me to lever him a little further away from my neck.

A split second later Jaclyn was there, ripping away the second cat an instant before she hit it with a double shot of electricity. Five minutes later the cats were all down from one or more shocks courtesy of Jaclyn, and the first of the cages were arriving.

We were all bloody, everyone except Grayson, but we'd managed not to lose anyone. As Brutus threw the last of the cats into a cage, I let my hybrid form shrink back down and hobbled over to Grayson.

"Thanks for seizing that last one there at the end of the fight. He had me dead to rights when you hit him."

Grayson shook his head. "I didn't do anything. He was the most resistant cat here and I had to choose between him and the two who were about to kill Arnold and Carson. I figured you for a goner."

A surge of rage exploded out from my beast, but I was even less interested than normal in trying to control its emotions. Before I could say something that Grayson would have to respond to, Carson was at my shoulder gently pulling me around.

"Let's get you out to one of the cars and get those arms looked at. We need to make sure that they are going to heal okay."

My beast shouldn't have allowed him to guide me out of the building, not as difficult as it had been lately, but his manner was so calm that I found myself unable to resist. We were all the way back to one of the SUVs before I started worrying that my beast's lack of resistance might mean that I'd been more seriously injured even than I'd realized.

Carson sat me on the curb and started taping me up like he'd played nurse dozens of times before.

"Try not to let Grayson get to you. He's always a little odd right after he gets done using his power like that. Don't be surprised if he apologizes for it later on."

My beast sent out a little pulse of anger but he seemed to be too tired to get truly worked up at this point.

"I know what I saw. One minute that cat was going to kill me and the next he was jerking around like he'd been electrocuted."

Carson held up his hands in a 'cool down' gesture. "Look I've been in a few dustups in my day. It's not uncommon for people to come back with wildly different versions of what happened, even experienced operators sometimes get a little stutter in the memory department when the adrenaline gets really flowing. I'm not saying you're wrong, I'm just saying that you were focused on your little corner and he was focused on his corner and the important thing is that we're all going to walk away from this particular mission."

It felt too dismissive, but I just couldn't seem to muster up the indignation that I should be feeling. That made me worry once again that I'd lost too much blood, but when I looked down Carson was already putting the finishing touches on my arms.

"I have to say you came out pretty lucky. I only caught bits and pieces of your fight, but I was sure that your arms were being torn to ribbons given the way those two were going at you. This isn't all that much worse than your typical sparring match."

"You're right, I'm not nearly as hurt as I thought I was. Maybe my memory is fuzzier than I realized."

Chapter 16

Adriana Paige
Graves Estate
Sanctuary, Utah

The wedding was just days away now, but I'd decided that I couldn't keep obsessing over it any more than I could keep obsessing over the gorgeous shape shifters who still threw themselves at Alec whenever they thought they could get away with it.

Things had died down slightly right after Lori had been sent home in a cage, but they'd been slowly ramping back up. Sooner or later Alec was going to have to put another of them in her place or he'd find himself with a lap full of lithesome blondes.

I pushed the thought away again and focused on what I had planned for the day. I was going to forget about the wedding and everything else and instead I was going to see if Rachel wanted to walk through the gardens.

Dominic looked up and smiled at me as I knocked on Rachel's door and then let myself in. Rachel didn't acknowledge my presence, but I'd come to realize that was the new normal.

"Hi, Dom. Can I take Rachel out to the garden?"

"Hello, Adri. Sure, I'll put her in her chair and go with you, just give me a minute to remember where I put her favorite jacket."

As Dom pulled herself to her feet I realized just how tired she was looking. It was as bad as before when Alec had been unconsciously draining everyone.

"Dom, you look terrible—are you getting any sleep?"

"Not quite as much as I should, but that isn't the main problem. My dreams have been really dark lately. It makes it so that I wake up not feeling very rested."

"If you can help me get Rachel ready then I can take her out into the garden. You should stay here and take a nap."

Dominic looked torn. "Alec will flip if Rachel doesn't have at least one bodyguard of her own."

I waved the concern away as I stepped back out into the hall. Carson looked over at me with a barely perceptible smile as soon as my head poked out of the room. He was still sporting some bandages from the excursion to capture the cats in Vegas, but he and most of the rest of the group had hopped on Alec's plane so they were back already.

The cages were still on their way back. The diesel was taking the long way home so as to avoid being stopped at a weigh station. Even Alec would have a hard time bribing enough people to cover up that kind of find.

"Carson, is there anyone you trust who's free right now so they could shadow Rachel while we are out in the garden?"

"I'm sure there is. I'll call into the ops room while you get Rachel ready to go."

"Thanks, Carson."

Dom was moving more slowly than normal and Rachel was completely passive, so it took nearly half an hour to get Rachel dressed in warmer clothes and situated in her wheelchair. James walked into the room a few minutes before we got done.

"I hear you need a hand."

Dominic looked like she was going to protest, but I beat her to the punch. "Yes, please, James. I just want to take Rachel out to the gardens on a walk and Dom needs to stay here and catch her breath."

"Perfect, let's go."

We left Dom with a frown on her face, but she stayed. As I pushed Rachel down the hall I spared a thought to hope that meant she'd be taking a nap.

Jasmin was waiting for us at the back door, Ben strapped limply into another wheelchair. "Do you mind if the two of us join you?"

I shook my head. "No, that would be fine. How did you know we'd be here?"

She tapped her earpiece. "I heard Carson asking for an extra body. I figured this might be good for Ben. You know, put him in different surroundings and provide some stimulation."

We'd been walking for less than twenty minutes before Kristin found us and asked if she could walk with us. We found a secluded corner of the garden that had a pair of stone benches and all stopped.

I tried for small talk with Kristin while I unbuckled Rachel and helped her out of her chair. After the second time of not getting a response to my queries, I waved a hand in front of Kristin's face.

"Are you okay?"

"Oh, yeah, sorry. I haven't been sleeping very well lately."

"There seems to be a lot of that going around lately."

Kristin shrugged with a nonchalance that I suspected she didn't actually feel. We weren't good enough buddies for her to seek me out like this without something else being up.

"It's not a big deal, at least I know what's causing it. It's got to be Dream Stealer again."

My mouth dropped open. Alec had mentioned that one of the Coun'hij had the ability to go into people's dreams, much like the power that Mallory said that I'd manifested, but I hadn't realized that he was still targeting Kristin like this.

"Kristin, that's a big deal. We need to tell Alec."

"Why, so he can throw me in a cage?"

I shook my head at her. "He's not going to throw you in a cage."

"Don't be so sure. Dream Stealer has driven people insane in the past. I just need to hold out for a few more days though. He tends to worry around at the edge of his target pack looking for the weak link. If I can last a little longer then he'll go looking for someone else to break. Don't worry, Ash is keeping a close eye on me."

It was a disturbing development, especially if Dom was up against the same kind of attack, but before I could decide what to say next James and Carson both stepped forward like they were going to try and get us out of the area.

Jasmin sighed and waved them back to their posts before they got to us. "No use trying to avoid a scene now, guys, not as long as it's going to take to get Rachel into her chair."

I looked over at Rachel, but she was completely lost in her own little world. She was currently watching invisible people walk back and forth in front of her. I was going to ask

Jasmin what she was talking about and then I heard them.

"...through talking to you about this, about anything."

"No, you're not. You don't understand what you're getting into. You don't even know him, not really."

"I know him better than I know you, but that's not important. The important thing is that he doesn't treat me like some kind of porcelain doll! He actually cares what I think about stuff."

They were moving our direction at a pretty good clip. I could recognize their voices now that they were closer and my heart went out to Jessica and Isaac. The last thing they needed was half a dozen witnesses to their drama.

The steps stopped abruptly, like maybe Isaac had grabbed hold of Jessica's arm.

"Jess...Jessica, I'm serious. If you don't want to be with me then that's fine, I can accept that. Wyatt isn't what he seems to be though. Carson told me something that makes me think that Wyatt isn't telling you the whole story. I mean how can he be? He appears out of nowhere, swears to Alec for two months and then he'll disappear again. You're going to get hurt."

I heard a meaty thunk, like Jess had slapped Isaac, and then the lighter set of footsteps headed our way again as she yelled back over her shoulder at him.

"You don't talk to me about Wyatt, ever. You're still just worried about your own ego and Carson is a meddling old woman who should be pushed out of a plane."

Jessica came crashing through the hedges that surrounded our little piece of the garden and went to go stomping through the middle of our group, but Rachel stepped up in front of her. When Jess tried to go around her, Rachel slapped her with every ounce of power she could generate.

If anyone else had done it Jess would have torn into them, but the action was so unexpected from Rachel, especially the new Rachel who hardly ever even recognized that there were other people around, that Jess just blinked at her for the couple of seconds it took for James to get between the two of them.

Carson was only a step behind James, and he restrained Jessica as James put Rachel back in her chair. I half expected Rachel to struggle, but she just looked sadly at Jessica and shook her head.

"'Show some respect. You shouldn't speak ill...well, you should just show some respect."

The weird stuff was piling up faster than you could shake a stick at it. I needed answers if I was going to help Alec hold everything together, but I didn't know where to turn for help anymore.

Chapter 17

Adriana Paige
Graves Estate
Sanctuary, Utah

I wasn't paying enough attention to what Carson was showing me and I knew it. We'd spent the last half hour walking through the park so that he could show me his progress with the flowers, and I'd only caught every third word or so.

I realized he was on to me when we ended up back at the golf cart and he ended his update with, "...it sounds like we're agreed then. I'll rip out all of the flowers and put in ornamental ponds instead."

I blushed as he looked at me with the barest hint of a twinkle in his eyes. "I'm sorry, Carson. You've been doing such incredible work out here and I didn't pay you anywhere near the attention that you deserved."

He gently shook his head at me. "There's no need to apologize. In all honesty, this is more for your sake than it is for mine. I wanted to give you one last chance to make any changes to the plans before the big day. I'm happy with how things have turned out, but that's all of little value if you're not equally happy with the results."

I shook my head and looked back out over the miniature greenhouses that had been constructed over most of the flower gardens. Nearly all of the plants that Carson had picked out were hardy enough to deal with what passed as winter in Sanctuary, but even so they wouldn't normally bloom until the warmer months of the year. The hothouses allowed him to control every aspect of their environment so that he could make sure they were perfect when the actual wedding arrived.

"If I wanted to change anything this late in the game then you should drag me in to get my head examined. We'd have to pay all kinds of overtime to move everything around by hand now because the rest of the park is finished enough that we can't bring in any kind of heavy equipment. Besides, nothing needs changing because you've done an absolutely amazing job. Visually it's gorgeous and while my nose is only human good, the scents seem equally divine. You deserve to have me say as much and you definitely deserve to have me pay attention while you show off your handiwork."

Carson looked over at Vivian, who was helping with my security for the day, and motioned towards the top of the bowl. "Give us a minute please, Vivian."

Rebekka's daughter nodded and started the long trudge to the rim of the amphitheater. Carson watched until she was out of hearing range and then looked around as if to confirm that nobody else was listening to us. We'd scheduled the outing during the time when the various landscaping crews took their lunch, so we had the park to ourselves.

"I meant what I said, Adri. More than anything else I just want you to be happy. Being able to serve the royal line in even a small way is more than a sufficient reward for my efforts. Would you like to talk about what's bothering you?"

"Is it that obvious?"

Carson bestowed another kind smile on me. Sometimes it was hard to remember that he was one of our top fighters. He was so even-keeled that he reminded me of an older, wiser version of Isaac before everything had come apart with Jess. Those qualities didn't usually go together with ruthless aggression when it came to life-and-death situations, but Carson somehow had them in spades.

It was nice that Alec had assigned me a bodyguard who not only was one of the more deadly fighters we had, but also seemed to genuinely care about me as a person.

"I don't think that anyone else realizes just how preoccupied you are, Adri, but I know you a little better than most."

I shrugged. "I guess you're right, the problem is that I almost don't even know where to start. Sometimes it seems like there is more wrong than right. Isaac, Jess and Wyatt are a constant source of drama, I have this huge wedding that is completely over the top in every way, and those two things aren't even at the top of the list."

I looked back in the direction of the house even though I couldn't see it, and sighed. "Rachel isn't herself anymore, Jasmin is unhappy all of the time, Ben is in a coma, and my mom is marrying Russ. It just feels like everything is in constant motion. How can I get my feet underneath me if events are rushing towards me faster than I can possibly deal with them?"

I let myself sit down in the golf cart and put my head in my hands. There were a few seconds of silence and then Carson lowered himself down onto the seat next to me and cleared his throat.

"I've wanted to be a gardener for as long as I can remember. You've been very complimentary about my work here in the park, but the truth of it is that I'm no more than a hobbyist. There is so much that I'd like to learn, but my time is spent learning how to kill people instead of creating beauty."

I felt a flash of guilt. A huge percentage of Carson's time was spent babysitting me and I'd never really thought about the fact that he might have something else that he'd rather be doing. Alec was paying him, but money didn't really matter, not against the kind of vocation that Carson had.

Carson seemed to read my mind. "There are good parts about what I do now, taking care of you for one, but when I look back over my life so much of it has been spent doing things that were important rather than doing the things that I wanted to do."

"I'm sorry, Carson. I never really thought about that. You've got a lot of time ahead of you though, right? I mean given that shape shifters live for so long you've got, what, another couple of hundred years at least? You could do a lot between now and then."

I looked up in time to see Carson shrug his shoulders. "The future is a path branching with endless possibilities, but I suspect that I'll never live to see peace arrive for my people. There will always be another group of monsters that need put down, another threat that needs dealt with. Unfortunately, for all that I love gardening, my true talents lie in other areas."

Carson smiled as he looked off into the distance and for a second I wondered what he was thinking about. His expression had changed there for a heartbeat into something gentler than I'd ever seen out of him before.

"My life hasn't been a waste though. I have a lot to be thankful for, a lot to be proud of, and I've learned a few things along the way."

There was another pause, almost as if Carson was searching for the right words. "If you would like, I'll let you in on the part of gardening that was the hardest for me to accept early on."

"Yes, please."

"The plants are going to do what the plants want to do. All you can do as a gardener is try to encourage the behavior you want, provide the best conditions possible and then wait to see what the plant does with what you've given it. People are the same way. Jess, Isaac and Wyatt will have to find their own path and the most that you can hope is that they will take advantage of the conditions here while they last."

I nodded as the meaning of his words started to sink in. "I guess that holds true with Jasmin and Rachel too. It's just so hard not being able to help them more right now. You would think that I'd be used to feeling powerless given that I'm surrounded by people who are all stronger and faster than me, but I hate this feeling."

Carson patted my arm. "That feeling is a good sign. The fact that you're feeling powerless now means that you've come to an understanding of just how much power you actually do wield. So many people go through life never realizing the extent of the influence they can exert through seemingly small things. They feel powerless all of the time, but this is a recent development for you, so it's a good thing."

I shrugged. "If you say so. It doesn't feel like it though."

"This feeling is a gift, especially for someone like you. You need to remember what it feels like so that when you are standing at Alec's side passing judgment on your people, you'll remember to be merciful."

Tears started pooling in my eyes. I shouldn't have been surprised that Carson had seen through to the thing that was bothering me most of all. He'd shown an incredible amount of insight already in the past.

"Carson, I don't want to be a queen. I don't want that kind of power. All I've ever wanted is to take care of my friends and family."

"I know, Adri. That's part of what makes you so special. You understand your power, but you don't love it for its own sake. All of the best gardeners are that way. You're starting down a path that will help you become one of those rare people who know how to cultivate others, how to nurture them, while still remembering that ultimately it's their choice what they will become."

"I suppose that it's too late to back out now."

It was a pretty feeble attempt at humor, but Carson seemed to sense the truth behind it. I didn't want to back out on Alec, but I woke up every morning wishing that Alec and I could just go off by ourselves without all of the concerns of running a pack or ruling the moonborn.

"As long as there is room for a choice it's never too late to make a change, Adri. In your case though, I suspect that making that kind of a change would run counter to your nature. I've seen people make those kinds of choices, but denying your fundamental character always leads to prolonged unhappiness. You may not realize it yet, but you've already started expanding your list of friends and family. Being queen is just that on a bigger scale. Don't worry though; you'll have time to grow into the role."

I reached out and wrapped both of my arms around Carson's arm, hugging it for all I was worth. "Thanks, Carson. Sometimes I don't know what I'd do without you."

"You'd be fine, Adri. It might take you a little bit longer to find your way, but you'd do it eventually. The good plants always do."

Chapter 18

Adriana Paige
Graves Estate
Sanctuary, Utah

I was somewhere completely new, but it somehow felt familiar at the same time. To my left was an inconceivably big tangle of thread that stretched back further than I could see. As I studied it in the dim light I realized that it wasn't so much a tangle as it was an infinite number of hair-fine threads that each moved from left to right and that, while the total assembly hung unsupported in the air, each individual thread was supported by tens of thousands of connections with other threads.

I tried to study the threads in front of me in more detail, but my mind shied away from looking too closely. I got vague impressions of individual threads, some magnificent with rich colors, others dull and frayed, but it seemed more than my consciousness could handle to actually take in the full measure of an individual thread.

Part of me wanted to force the issue, to pick a single thread and focus all of my attention on it, but something below the level of sentience refused to let me proceed. Frustrated with my inability to make sense of what I was seeing, I instead looked to the right and felt my sanity start to unravel in the split second before primitive survival instincts forced my eyes closed.

The threads that had been a weighty mass off to my left became something different when they passed me and went the other direction. They didn't have substance anymore, instead they were shadows cast by a million points of light. They expanded to take up more space than existed in the entire universe, or maybe they simply disappeared into dimensions that my mind wasn't ready to know existed.

The only thing that had been solid, that had seemed real, in the vista that had expanded out before me had been the tired figure of a man who'd been struggling to cut a single thread free of its neighbors.

He looked different here, but I somehow knew that this was the same man who had saved Isaac, Jasmin and me from the werewolf in New York.

"Where am I, what am I looking at?"

My eyes were still closed, but I could hear the laughter in his voice. "I was about to ask you the same thing. It's different, you know, for each person. None of us can see it in its entirety, so we all put up artificial constructs to protect ourselves. Even me, even after all of these years."

The laughter that had been dancing behind his voice momentarily leaked over into the real thing, but this laughter that had an element of hysteria to it. He cut off the sound almost before I'd realized how disturbing it was, but it echoed through my mind even after he'd become silent again.

"It would be interesting to know what you saw, but that will have to wait for another time. It's risky for you to be here. Go back to Alec and tell him not to bother with trying to track the cats down."

"What do you mean?"

"There's no time, Adri. Just remember to tell him. Tell him that and tell him that the three must go their separate ways."

I was thrust back into the waking world with a suddenness that left my heart racing, but I pulled myself out of bed and stumbled over to the door out to the hall, still in my pajamas. Carson was still faithfully standing next to my door when I opened it.

"Are you okay, Adri?"

"I'm not sure. I need to find Alec though. Can you please see if anyone knows where he is?"

"He's in Donovan's office. Things are pretty chaotic right now. The trailer with the cats just arrived but they escaped somehow."

I took a deep breath and then nodded. "Even more reason to get me there sooner rather than later. Let me throw some clothes on so that people will take me seriously."

Less than fifteen minutes later Carson and I were standing outside Donovan's office. I knocked on the door and felt a pulse of power as someone throttled back irritation at the interruption.

Donovan answered the door and then stepped to the side to allow me to enter.

"I just had a dream where someone told me that the cats were going to escape and that we shouldn't try to track them down."

I managed to get it all out before anyone managed to interrupt and then I looked around to see who was present.

Alec was sitting behind Donovan's desk with Ash in the seat closest. Jaclyn shook her head as Donovan pulled the door shut again. "The only way for someone to have sent you some kind of message already was if they engineered the escape."

Ash shook his head. "Technically we don't know when they actually disappeared on us. It could have been mere minutes or it could have been hours ago."

I held up a hand. "What happened?"

Alec rubbed his temples as he answered. "Nobody knows, not really. Peter and Rex were the two who were driving the truck back. They both swear that they only ever stopped for food and gas, and that even then they worked in shifts to make sure that the cages were never left unguarded."

"There's no evidence of any kind of tampering on the truck?"

Ash looked over at Jaclyn for confirmation, but it was obvious that he already knew she was going to shake her head. "No, there's nothing physically wrong with the cages or the trailer. The locks are all still in place and I checked that they still work with the original keys that Peter had on him."

A half-formed thought tickled the back of my mind. I couldn't pin it down to anything specific, but a question tumbled out of my mouth almost without conscious effort on my part.

"What about Peter and Rex? Are there any kind of physical clues there?"

Jaclyn looked at me oddly for several seconds before nodding. "Maybe. Peter has a gash on his arm that he doesn't remember getting. It's not a major wound, but it struck me as odd that he didn't remember a two-inch-long cut."

"Are there any hybrids who are known to have the ability to walk through walls?"

Jaclyn shook her head. "No, I'm not even sure something like that is possible, no matter how powerful someone is."

Alec waved us all quiet. "This isn't getting us anywhere. Absent a known suspect who can somehow manipulate space and time, we aren't going to be able to track the missing cats down. For now, I think that Adri's mystery messenger was right. There isn't any point wasting time and effort pursuing them, not with everything else we have going on. We just need to remember that whoever was in your dream is probably working with whoever took our missing cats, and both of them are probably going to continue to work against us."

I opened my mouth to tell Alec that it had been the old man, the priest, who'd saved Jasmin, Isaac and me from the werewolf, and then shut it without saying anything. I didn't have any reason to distrust anyone present, but something wouldn't let me say it. Until I knew more about this mysterious priest I wasn't going to draw any more attention to him than I had to.

Chapter 19

Alec Graves
Graves Estate
Sanctuary, Utah

Tasha didn't look happy to see me, but she'd shown up to the briefing, so I didn't complain. Jaclyn arrived a few seconds later and shut the door to my new office. Donovan had paid some pretty hefty fees to get my dad's old office refurbished in just two weeks, but getting access to some more secure, usable space would have been worth at least four or five times as much as what he'd actually ended up having to pay.

Jaclyn sank down into one of the plush leather chairs and then we both turned to Tasha. She didn't seem keen to volunteer anything so I cleared my throat.

"Have you been getting the cooperation you need out of the other packs?"

"Yes. I got a little bit of static from the Flagstaff pack right after they joined up, but Mom helped get them to toe the line for me."

I nodded and leaned back in my chair. "Good, I'm glad to hear it. You indicated that you thought you had enough information to make this meeting worthwhile, so go ahead and tell the two of us what you've found."

Tasha took a deep breath and then started. "Nobody has anything solid on the ghost pack, but I'm starting to see a pattern. Every time I get close to someone who is supposed to have actually talked to one of these guys they get really quiet about where they were when it all happened."

Jaclyn tapped her finger against her chair. "So they were probably east of the Mississippi. That's not surprising. If you were going to try and hide a pack you'd almost have to put them in the prohibited area."

Tasha pulled out two file folders and tossed one to each of us. "I've got a map in there with all of the reported encounters on it, but the really interesting bit is the list of supposed powers that I've been able to start pulling together. The first page is everything I've heard even once. The second page cross-references the powers with any description I was able to connect to the individuals with the powers. I've started to create a list of pack members and their likely powers."

I flipped to the second page and a low whistle escaped me. "Group paralysis. That sounds familiar, doesn't it?"

Jaclyn found the entry I was looking at and frowned. "So you're saying that Grayson is part of the ghost pack?"

"No, that's what I thought at first too, but when you look at the heat map of the sightings you see that there are two epicenters. Grayson might be part of the ghost pack, but it's more likely that he's part of this second group which I think is based somewhere in Florida."

My beast chose that moment to act up, but I got ahead of it and stopped it from completing the transformation. I wouldn't have expected a casual observer to have understood the sudden flash of anger, but Tasha surprised me with her bitter smile.

"Exactly, we've been doing this to ourselves. There is a goldmine of information out there but the various packs have never trusted each other enough to pull it together into anything useful. The Coun'hij has kept control over our entire race simply by keeping us at each other's throats."

I made a throwing-away gesture. "We're doing what we can to change that but it's going to take some time. I'll talk to Grayson and see if I can get some kind of confirmation out of him as to which group he's in, but for now let's assume that Grayson isn't part of the ghost pack, and that his group is the one in Florida. Where does that leave us?"

"Flying mostly in the dark, if I'm totally honest with you. Grayson's group is the one that is the most active, so I have more data on them, but even that isn't saying much."

It had taken me longer than it should have, but I was getting the hang of how she'd organized the data. I flipped back to the list of powers and found the section that dealt with the ghost pack.

"These two are the important ones. Tracking and speed. The speed guy is the pack's alpha."

Jaclyn looked at me consideringly. "What makes you think so?"

"Every rumor I've heard has been in agreement that the alpha of the ghost pack is unbeatable. Some of these powers are impressive, but none of them are as dangerous as pure unadulterated speed."

Tasha didn't look convinced. "Some of these are pretty intense, Alec. I've got everything from invisibility to some kind of Jedi mind control. Do you really think speed trumps all of that?"

"You're right, some of this stuff is more powerful, but your average shape shifter doesn't think that way. I'm not talking two-minute-mile fast, I'm talking you-never-even-see-the-blow-coming fast. If someone was really that fast they could kill me or Grayson, or even your mom, before we could even react."

Jaclyn frowned, not at my explanation, but at the implications. She'd been the king of the hill for decades, but new threats were practically falling out of the sky these days.

"You wanted me here because you're sending me in against that?"

I gave her a tired smile. "I'm not asking you to go in and kill the entire pack singlehandedly, but yes, you're my best bet for finding them."

"What if they decide that they don't want to just talk? If this guy is as fast as you think he is then I won't even stand a chance."

I'd known that Jaclyn was probably going to bring that point up, and I'd been debating the best response for a couple of days now.

"I have it on good authority that you haven't reached the extent of what your power could actually be. I think that you should spend some time trying to expand what you're capable of. If you generate a standing field and make it strong enough, then anyone physically attacking you would be knocked down. It wouldn't matter how fast he was."

I could see the wheels turning in her head. My statement wasn't proof that Mallory was still alive. It was always possible that she'd told Donovan before she'd been killed and that he'd then passed the information on to me. It was possible, but it was incredibly unlikely and Donovan said that there had been rumors for years that Mallory hadn't actually been killed when Agony had come to town.

"How good is your authority?"

"It's extremely good authority, Jaclyn, and that's all that I can tell you for now."

She considered my response for several seconds before nodding. "Okay. I'll go. How much help are you going to send along with me?"

"I'm open to requests."

"Okay, let me spend the afternoon thinking about it. I'll get back to you tonight with a proposal and we can get started first thing tomorrow."

I stood and shook her hand before she left. "Thank you for doing this, Jaclyn. This is incredibly important. We need to find the Coun'hij and we need to find them soon. Best case you find this tracker guy and he tells us exactly where to find Puppeteer and the rest. If you can't find him and recruit him to our cause then I've either got to get my hands on a southerner who can track and then lure one of the Coun'hij into place so that he can track them, or I've got to hope that the Coun'hij makes a mistake that will let us track them back using more conventional means."

"I understand. I'll do my very best."

It wasn't until after Jaclyn had been gone for nearly a minute that Tasha stood up and walked over to my desk.

"So what do I do now?"

"Keep doing what you've been doing. With any luck we should have more packs joining us in the next few days. I want you to continue to correlate as much information as you can and stay in touch with your mom so that she's as well armed as possible."

"What about after that?"

I sighed and put down her report. "I meant what I said, Tasha. I'll keep you in an advisory position and make sure that you're not sucked into all of the petty dominance crap."

"And if I want more than that?"

"You're not my slave, Tasha. If you want something else then go for it. I'm not going to stop you."

"What if what I want is you?"

"That's just as much off the table now as it was the last time we talked. I love Adri and that isn't going to change. Find someone who can love you like you deserve."

She shook her head at me. "I'm not stupid. Any idea that love might enter into things went by the wayside a little while ago. When I marry it will be because I've finally found someone who can protect me from all of the threats out there."

"There's more than just physical security to a relationship, Tasha."

"Not for me there isn't."

Chapter 20

Jasmin Bianchi
Sanctuary Airport
Sanctuary, Utah

The estate was a complete zoo, but that was all magnified a hundred fold here in the hangars where both of Alec's planes were housed when they weren't in the air. Donovan, and Ash were doing the best they could to make sure that all of the logistics were running smoothly, but there was no way to organize an operation of this size without a few hiccups along the way.

There'd been plenty of debate about whether or not to believe Dominic's contact, but in the end Alec had decided that it was just too good of an opportunity to pass up, so we were headed to the other circle on Dom's map and we were going loaded for bear.

Alec was staying to protect the non-combatants, who included more than just Addison, Andrew, Rachel, Adri and his mom these days. He'd flown all of the non-fighters in to Sanctuary and he was keeping a handful of wolves and hybrids back to help him hold down the fort, but everyone else was gearing up for the largest excursion since shortly after the border wars when we'd kicked the cats back down into South America.

Jaclyn had disappeared a couple of days ago, but I was pretty sure that she'd been sent off on some kind of mission by Alec. She wouldn't have been much if any extra use if we were really going up against werewolves like we were expecting to, but it still would have been nice to have her along. She'd seen more combat than just about any of the other alphas. A couple of the other border packs had mixed things up just as much against the cats, but Jaclyn's pack was the only one that had been so active when it came to hunting down werewolves.

Even without the ability to drop them with a million volts of electricity, she still would have been a definite asset to have around. Instead we were going in with old-fashioned muscle power to deal with any werewolves and Grayson to back us up if this turned out to be some kind of trap.

I knew Alec wanted to be in on the fight, but I couldn't argue with the logic that kept him here in Sanctuary and sent Grayson out in his place. Alec was good, but once he dropped a group of shifters then he was the only one who could go in and put them down without being caught up in the draining effect of his ability.

Grayson on the other hand was selective enough that he could drop a dozen or so of the bad guys and keep them down while the rest of us delivered the coup de grâce. Even so, I would have felt a lot better if it had been Alec with us rather than Grayson. The terrible trio had always seemed a little bit off to me, but Grayson was far and away the most creepy of the three. There had been something about the way he'd acted after the fights with the cats that had rubbed me the wrong way. I'd never seen anyone so emotionless, especially not after telling someone else that they'd been ready to sacrifice them.

Isaac wasn't the controlled pillar he'd been in years past, but even at his best he'd never been like this. Grayson hadn't just been controlled, he'd been a blank slate. I couldn't think of anything more unnatural, not for a shape shifter. Emotion was what drove us. Intellect might direct our routes, but it was emotion that kept us going in the face of odds that would make most humans give up and die.

I still didn't know what Grayson's deal was, but there was something very off about him.

Somebody was making a bunch of noise over by the main entrance. I didn't have to check and recheck my gear like Ash and a couple of the others, so I drifted over to see what all of the excitement was about. I was beyond bored. Once we hit the ground and the fur and fangs were flying then I'd be missing the boredom, but right now I was even willing to listen to some of the ridiculous drama going on in the pack lately if it would break up the monotony.

Wyatt was standing in the doorway arguing with Carson. Grayson was watching impassively from a few feet away, which was yet another oddity. No dominant hybrid should watch quite so calmly when one of his guys was defying orders, even if the orders weren't actually his orders.

"Rex agreed to stay and watch Rachel, so there isn't any good reason for me to sit this one out."

"You know very well why you should be sitting this fight out. You have responsibilities that you shouldn't be forgetting."

"That's crap and you know it. I could get offed tomorrow and it wouldn't make one damn bit of difference."

"You agreed to obey Alec's orders. He told you to stay at the estate."

"I already know that Alec assigned me as a babysitter specifically because you asked him to keep me out of the exciting stuff. I just told him that Rex would watch the kids and he told me it was up to you two, so here I am."

Carson didn't look happy, but he also didn't seem willing to lay all of his cards on the table, not with everyone else around at least.

"Think of what your grandfather would say."

"He'd say that our line should have died out centuries ago."

Wyatt pushed past Carson as he spoke and apparently his shot succeeded because neither Carson or Grayson made any motion to stop him.

It was pretty apparent that the show was over, so I drifted back to the far corner of the hangar where I'd been sitting before Wyatt showed up. It had the benefit of being far enough out of the way that most people had been leaving me alone.

My thoughts lapsed back into their normal, well-worn grooves once I was back by myself. I already knew that there wasn't a single thing I could do to help Ben at this point, but that didn't stop me from banging my head against that particular wall over and over again.

It was darkly funny when you got right down to it. Ben had left town because I'd addicted him to my touch. It hadn't been on purpose, and I hadn't had any other choice, at least not one that kept him alive, but he hadn't been able to deal with it.

What he hadn't realized was that he'd addicted me years before any of that had happened. I'd spent years trying to get him to just stop moving around so that I could sit him down and get him to listen to me, and now he was finally stuck in one place and I still couldn't talk to him. Rather I could talk to him, but it wasn't doing any good.

I was mentally reviewing the results of his last test when I heard someone behind me. I spun around and had Rachel up against the wall with my hand on her throat before I realized who I was dealing with.

"Rach, how did you even get here?"

The question was pure habit. I didn't really expect an answer out of her. These days she mostly just ignored all of us.

"Rex is nice, but he's not the brightest cookie out there. I lost him twenty minutes ago. Once he was out of the picture it was easy to steal the keys to my car and the key to the back door here."

"Don't you mean brightest lightbulb?"

Her shrug didn't fool me. She was smiling because she was yanking my chain.

"I don't have much longer, Jasmin. Alec's looking for me already."

"You're right, he's probably freaking out by now. We should call him and tell him that you're okay."

I'd let go of her as soon as I'd realized I wasn't being attacked, but suddenly I wasn't so sure. Rachel stepped into me with a hiss of frustration. "You're not listening to me, Jas. I need you to listen because you're important to me. This is important."

My beast awakened with a flare of power. She knew Rach, but she'd been acting up a lot lately and she apparently felt like Alec's little sister was suddenly a big threat.

"Okay, Rach. I'm listening."

"You need to find someone named Geoffrey and you'll need to find him soon. Ben doesn't have much longer."

"Wait, this Geoffrey guy can help Ben?"

"Yes, but you're not going to like it."

"How do I find him?"

Her odd smile was back, the one that usually meant that she was inhabiting a different place or time than the rest of us.

"Don't worry about that, it will happen; you just need to be ready when he does."

It was all I could do not to reach out and shake Rachel. There was no reason to believe that she knew any more about how to save Ben than I did, but I needed it to be true and I needed her to keep things together long enough to tell me whatever it was that she knew.

"Mind the smell, Jas. Mind the smell."

There were footsteps behind us now, but I ignored them right up until someone put a hand on my shoulder and started pulling me back away from Rachel. Somehow I'd ended up with my hand back around her throat.

"Just let go of her, Jasmin."

It was James and he was talking with unusual calm, but that didn't matter.

"Tell me what you know, Rachel!"

"I can't tell you, I'd have to show you and if I did that you wouldn't thank me, nobody would."

My beast felt like she was being made fun of and she didn't like the experience. She tried to break free and it was all I could do to keep her from shedding my normal form in favor of the four-legged one.

I was so caught up with aborting the transformation that I didn't realize I was hurting Rachel until she cried out and James had thrown me against one of the metal struts that supported the structure.

Tears of pain were running down Rachel's face and she had vivid purple bruises on her shoulder and neck, but she was laughing hysterically. "That's the ticket, Jas. Give into the rage, use it. You're going to need it, all of it, before this is all over."

Chapter 21

Adriana Paige
Graves Estate
Sanctuary, Utah

I knew that I shouldn't be bothering Alec, not with everything else he had going on right now, but that didn't stop me from walking to his office. The wedding was just next week and the work involved in getting ready for it was growing in step with the passage of time. Kami was amazing, but a thousand things still went wrong every day. It meant that we were in a perpetual firefighting mode as we tried to come up with ways to compensate.

Things would have been much easier if I hadn't tried to cram six months of planning and work into such a short period of time, but it was still starting to wear on me. Alec and I usually at least had breakfast and dinner together each day, but today I was feeling the need for a little more Alec time.

I looked back at one of Rebekka's wolves, a quiet guy named Jed who was currently serving as my bodyguard, and then shrugged. "I guess I should just knock. It's not like he's going to turn me away."

Jed smiled slightly. "I suspect he'll be as relieved to see you as you will be to see him."

I rolled my eyes and then knocked on the door. Alec answered it a moment later with a frown on his face that turned to a smile as soon as he saw that it was me who was interrupting his work.

"You have no idea how good it is to see you right now."

"I don't know, I think I'm feeling about the same way."

He pulled me into a hug and then looked over at Jed. "You can go ahead and take a break. I'll give you a call when Adri is ready to leave."

"Yes, sir."

Alec pulled me into his office and swung the door shut. "You're never going to guess who ditched her minder and snuck off the estate."

"When you put it that way, it's not hard to figure it out. Your mom and Rachel are the only two besides me who have constant bodyguards. Have you found Rachel yet?"

I wondered briefly if I should have been more worried, but Alec seemed more annoyed than upset, so I figured that meant that they'd already found her.

"Yeah, but only because she went to the airstrip where our people were assembling for the attack on the werewolves in Salt Lake. If she'd just chosen to keep driving we might not have ever found her. Tracking a vehicle is tough because it doesn't have a very distinctive scent trail, and we've lost our satellite feeds for this area."

I rubbed my arms. "That sounds serious. Not just the Rachel thing, but the satellite feeds. Do you think it's the precursor of an attack?"

Alec's frown told me that he'd already spent the odd hour or two worrying about that very thing. "I don't know. We don't have our own satellites, so we've relied on hacks into the NSA and others to get the surveillance that we need. Every so often they scrub their systems enough to deny us access, so this happens from time to time, but frankly the timing isn't good. Especially not with how odd one of our cyber consultants has been behaving lately."

"What do you mean?"

"It's hard to really pin these guys down sometimes, but he seems to be racking up a lot of extra hours lately and he's been late delivering his normal stuff, like he's working on something high priority for someone else despite the fact that he's only supposed to be working for me."

I smiled as he pulled me down onto the loveseat next to him. "The joys of running a multibillion-dollar empire that happens to be in the middle of overthrowing the Coun'hij."

Alec snorted and took my hand in his own. "At least Rachel is on her way back here. She should be here within the next ten minutes or so."

"Traffic permitting, of course."

I got another eye roll and then Alec used his free hand to bring my chin up ever so slightly.

"I've missed you today."

"You saw me just a few hours ago."

His smile was sad. "I know, but somehow that feels like days ago. On days like this it's the thought of seeing you at breakfast that convinces me to push through the night and get the work done. I hate having something unfinished hanging over my head when I'm trying to enjoy your company."

"If it helps any, I've missed you terribly tonight too. I'd give anything to have all of this craziness behind us. I wish the wedding were tomorrow, but if I really had less than twenty-four hours to pull everything else together then I'd probably steal one of Ash's guns and shoot myself."

"We could try and push the date back a month or two if that would help."

I shuddered in terror that was only half feigned. "I've seen the guest list, Alec. We've invited three different state governors, six senators and something like two dozen other people who plan out their schedules four months in advance. Besides, changing the date at this point would be a lot of work. Kami has shipments queued up to arrive according to a very precise schedule every day between now and the actual wedding. The only thing that a delay would actually do is give us more time to get the park ready to go."

"If all you're worried about at this point is the park then you can stop worrying. I snuck out there yesterday and it is perfect. You guys have created something that's almost too good to survive in this world. The flowers are especially incredible. Carson has a true gift, both for the visuals and for the scents."

I shook my head. "I can't take any credit for the park. I haven't actually done any work anywhere since this whole nightmare started."

I'd looked down in unhappiness while we'd been talking, but Alec tipped my chin back up so that I'd meet his eyes.

"In some ways you and Kami have the hardest jobs of all. You have the ultimate responsibility if things go wrong. Besides, you should give yourself credit for agreeing to let Carson do the flowers. You recognized talent and gave him his head. Not only that, I have it on very good authority that you were the one who gave him the idea of using Lagrimas so liberally throughout the park."

"I don't know. That doesn't seem like a very big accomplishment. Besides, if we're giving out credit for putting the right person in the right time and place, you need a healthy dose of applause. Carson has been perfect, and not just with the flowers. I didn't realize just how much of an adjustment it was going to be to have a bodyguard all of the time rather than just a few hours a day. I know it's only been a couple of months, but Carson has almost become like an adopted father."

I knew Alec's sigh wasn't because of the bond Carson and I had developed, but it took several seconds before he nodded and elaborated on the gesture.

"I'm glad that things have worked out so well there, but that's one more bit of unfinished business. Carson and the other two are almost to the end of their sworn period of service and I haven't managed to tease anything important out of any of them. If I can't get through to them soon they are going to disappear again and then I'll be looking at trying to replace not only Carson as your bodyguard, but Grayson as well."

"It will leave us a lot weaker, won't it?"

"Yes. It's not like it's the end of the world. We've got several packs that have sworn to us now, so we've got more manpower than we had before, but he's still going to leave a hole around here when he leaves."

I'd nearly forgotten about the time limit on Carson's oath to Alec, and I felt a sudden flare of sadness at the thought of him disappearing from my life. "I'll do what I can to see if he'll open up to me. I don't want him and the others to leave any more than you do."

I opened my mouth to ask him how things were looking with some of the packs that we hoped would swear to us next, but shut it when I realized that the sliver of white that I could see under the corner of Alec's desk was a note, and that it had my name on it.

"You're leaving me notes in unlikely places now?"

Alec followed my gaze and then shook his head as he walked over and picked it up. "No, this isn't from me and it has my name on the other side of the envelope."

"So it's for both of us. Go ahead and open it—the suspense is killing me."

Alec tore the envelope open and scanned down the page. By the time he got to the bottom of the note he was white. He pulled his cell phone out as he tossed the note to me.

I read it as he paced back and forth, muttering under his breath as he waited for whoever he was calling to pick up.

Alec, Adri,

I'm sorry that you're going to find out like this, but I think it's best, all things considered. Don't follow me, and don't be too hard on Rex, there really isn't any way he could have seen this coming.

"Donovan, I need you to call the police. Have them put out an APB for whatever Rachel drove out to the hangar and whatever Rex used to go get her, and then get in contact with our IT assets. I need satellite from the last two hours and I need it yesterday."

Speaking of Rex, you should probably send someone to pick him up. He's on the side of the road about ten minutes outside of town. I shot him up with Etorphine, so if you give him some Revivon he'll be back on his feet by the time you need him.

Jasmin is going to be pissed when she gets back, but you need to go easy on her. She's having a hard time of things right now, but you're going to need her.

I think it's past time to bring certain secrets, certain people, out into the open, Alec. Adri, I'm sorry I haven't been able to help with the wedding. You two take care of each other, the worst is still to come.

By the time I made it to the end of Rachel's note, Alec had hung up on Donovan and was talking into one of the radios that was hooked into the net the bodyguards were using.

"...no, not everyone, we still have to make sure that we've got adequate protection for everyone else here. Detach four guys in two cars. She said that she'd leave Rex ten minutes outside of town, but she didn't say on which side and there's no guarantee that things went according to her plan. With any luck he overpowered her and his radio got turned off in the struggle. No, I don't think it's likely either, but I'd kill for a little bit of luck right now. Get ahold of Grayson for me too. I don't want them to do anything stupid, but tell them we're going to need them back here as soon as possible."

Alec set the radio down and walked back over to me. I held out the note and let him read it again.

"Do you think she's really gone?"

"Probably. There's always a chance that it's some kind of elaborate joke, but I doubt it."

"What do you think she meant about bringing secrets out into the open?"

"She's talking about something that she can't possibly know about, something that I should have done a long time ago."

I would have asked him what he meant, but he'd already turned away, absently pulling his phone back out of his pocket. He stared at it for several seconds and then hit Donovan's speed dial.

"Can you please let the police know to contact me directly with any updates? The same with the cyber guys...no, no problems, I just have another job for you to do. Hold on a sec, I need to tell Adri."

Alec looked over at me. "The police just found Rex. He was unconscious on the side of the road, just like Rachel's note said he would be. She's definitely gone."

It was like I'd been struck. I'd known that this was a possibility, but even with the note I'd still had a hard time believing that Rachel—even the new, unpredictable Rachel—could have really left like that. I crossed over to Alec and took his hand.

He gave me a sad smile and then turned back to his phone. "Donovan, I'd like you to take the Hummer and go get Mallory. Don't worry about leaving a trail, it's time for her to come home."

Chapter 22

Donovan Harringsford
Highway 112
Sanctuary, Utah

The night had taken on an undeniably surreal feeling. First Master Alec had informed me that Mistress Rachel had disappeared and then he'd ordered me into one of the vehicles and granted me the deepest desire of my heart.

It was nothing less than ridiculous, but I couldn't stop from feeling slightly guilty. The byzantine pathways in my mind seemed to have linked the two events. I knew they were unrelated, but what if I was wrong, what if my joy had only been possible because it was balanced by the tragedy of Mistress Rachel abandoning us?

On any other day my attention would have been wholly focused on the road. I did so little driving that each time I manned the wheel of one of the fantastical beasts that filled the garage it felt as though I was taking my life into my own hands. Tonight was different, almost as though my mind was flittering about in an effort to not focus on my purpose. It was like one of those dreams where you approached your destination slowly because you knew that once you arrived you'd wake up and you couldn't bear to have the dream end any sooner than it had to.

I took myself to task once again and brought the vehicle's speed back up to something that would allow me to return home to the estate sometime before sunrise. This might be the moment that I'd yearned for countless times over the last two decades, but that didn't excuse me from my duties. Master Alec would doubtless require my assistance with the effort to find his sister.

Just ahead, barely visible because of the Hummer's powerful headlights, was the shed where Alec stored his motorcycle when he came for a visit. I slowed the vehicle and then turned to the right, bringing it gently off of the road and onto the barren land that concealed more than any casual observer would have realized.

My progress was painfully slow, but still much better than I could have managed by foot. Alec had selected the vehicle most able to make the journey, but even so nearly half an hour passed before I finally saw the entrance to the shallow cave that contained Mallory's home.

I brought the vehicle to a halt and turned it off without any conscious memory of having done so, and then found myself standing less than a pace from Mallory's door. Part of me still wished to prolong the moment, but I knew that she would be worried. Alec never would have arrived in such a fashion, so she likely assumed that our enemies had finally found her. I tugged my suit jacket into place and knocked on the door.

I schooled my features into a shadow of their normal proper expression and then waited as she crossed the distance between us and then opened the door.

"D...Donovan. Is it really you or am I caught up in a dream again?"

"If it's a dream then I'm trapped in the same one. I say trapped, but I mean favored. Master Alec instructed me to come retrieve you. He believes that it is past time for you to come out of the shadows and take your rightful place at his side."

Her fragile body, wrapped as it was in a simple dress, was a pale reflection of what it had been before Agony had crippled it, but it was a beautiful improvement over what she'd been like when I'd left her here so many years ago. Then she'd been bloodied and a bare couple of steps from death.

She looked at me out of the corner of her eye with the doubtful look I remembered from the time before Agony's first visit. "Alec didn't really say that, did he?"

"It was implied. Master Alec didn't actually need to say the words for me to know how he felt in this instance."

"I asked him to give me some time to think about his proposal, but I didn't expect him to be gone for so long. I've spent the last several weeks alternately hoping for and dreading his next visit. The last thing I expected was that he would send you here and take my choice away."

"Master Alec is coming into his inheritance. It is his to command and ours to obey, but you still have a choice, that is never really taken from you."

She smiled at me. "As you say. It would have been better for me to have said that he knows my heart as well as he knows yours. If he commands then I'll obey out of love for him. It's my heart that leaves me no choice."

I struggled to keep the hope out of my voice. "You'll come then?"

"I'm scared, Donovan. I'm not what I once was. The last twenty years have taken more from me than I ever would have believed possible. What if I fail Alec just like I failed his father?"

"Master Kaleb would never have agreed that you failed him."

"Wouldn't he? He made a choice to trade his life for yours, but I wasn't ready to see him go so

I pulled nearly the entire pack into a fight that we couldn't win. It's taken me a lot of years to realize it, but I did fail Kaleb."

I shook my head at her but she wasn't done.

"As sorry as I am for that, as much as I don't want to fail, Alec, I'm more worried that I'll fail you, Donovan. We've spent so long like this, a world apart. Are we really going to be able to make things work when we see each other every day?"

I gently took her hand and put it on my arm. She didn't resist as I slowly led her back towards the Hummer.

"I don't have any answers about the future, but I do know that the question is one that is entirely within your control. I loved you for more than two decades before Master Kaleb's death. I will continue to love you regardless of our circumstances."

Chapter 23

Alec Graves
Graves Estate
Sanctuary, Utah

I felt like I was going to lose my mind. Adri's presence was the only thing keeping me from going over the edge.

Nobody had seen any sign of Rachel and there wasn't anything else I could realistically do to find her at this point. We didn't have enough spare manpower right now to conduct some kind of massive search, not without leaving the estate completely exposed, and it probably wouldn't have helped even if we had a thousand people to send out in cars looking for her.

It had taken a tremendous act of will, but I'd done all that I could and then I forced Rachel's situation out of my mind and went back to my room. Adri had come with me and we'd spent the last two hours cuddled together on my bed while I waited for updates from Grayson's team or some kind of response out of the IT guys that Donovan had been chasing before I'd sent him to go get Mallory.

"Alec, what's going to happen after we get married? We can't really leave for a honeymoon or anything, can we?"

"It wouldn't be a very good idea. We'd be leaving everyone here exposed and we'd be in more than a little danger if we were off in some tropical paradise without any bodyguards."

Adri turned around so that she was facing me. "So what are we doing instead?"

"Who says that we're doing anything after the wedding?"

She rolled her eyes at me. "Please. I know you much too well to believe that for a moment. You've got something planned and I want to know what it is."

"You don't want to be surprised?"

"No, surprises aren't what everyone makes them out to be. I'd rather know what's coming."

I gave her a moment to reconsider and then nodded. "You're right, I have something planned. You haven't noticed, not with all of the craziness of getting the wedding ready to go, but there's been another construction project underway since just after we flew back from Chicago. Everything is on schedule for us to spend our first night as man and wife together in a small cabin that I've been wanting to have built for a few months now. The original it's based on was located in much colder environs, but I'm still very happy with how things are turning out."

Adri smiled and then buried her face in my chest. "That's perfect, Alec. A tiny little house where we can pretend for at least a few days that we're just two newlyweds, two normal, poor newlyweds."

"Maybe I should clarify what I meant by small..."

Adri didn't look entirely happy, but her response was preempted by a chirp from my phone which was followed by another message a couple of seconds later. The first one was from Grayson to inform me that they'd touched down in Sanctuary. Grayson had already indicated that he hadn't lost anyone and I'd been enjoying being alone with Adri so much that I'd resisted the urge to call and get a report on their operation, but it looked like our peaceful interlude was about to come to an end.

I was just about to call Grayson when I saw the second message. It was just a phone number, but the numeric code behind it told me that it was from the hacker who'd been so unreliable lately.

I took a deep breath and then dialed the number. The voice on the other end was being run through some kind of filter to make it unrecognizable.

"This is Alec, where have you been for the last six hours?"

"What do you mean where have I been? I've been doing exactly what you told me to do, I've been sitting inside the NSA's systems and doing everything I could to foil whoever is trying to hack in right now. By the way, everything I've been doing lately is way over what we agreed on two years ago when you hired me. I'm on the ragged edge of being caught here and you're going to get one hell of a bill when I actually have a few minutes to draw one up."

A shiver worked its way up my back. "I never told you to protect the NSA. I've had every other available resource trying to hack in so I could get access to their satellite feeds."

There was complete silence on the other end of the line for several seconds. "I got a message in the usual way four weeks ago telling me to hack in and shred all of the satellite feeds for a six-hour window that just ended. That data is gone, not even I could get it back at this point."

I felt a headache coming on. "Was there anything in the message that would have tipped you off to the fact that it wasn't coming from me?"

"No, the headers all originated from your network and you had all of the agreed-on codes and encryption in place. Given all of that, how was I supposed to know that it wasn't you? Even the odd bit at the end of the message didn't matter, not against all of the other proofs I had that it *was* you."

"What was at the end of the message?"

"I don't know, not exactly, I'd have to go dig it back up. Something about this secret remaining in the dark still."

I closed my eyes for a moment as I tried to keep my temper from getting away from me. "Please dig the message up and send it to me. Once you've done that go ahead and start reversing your efforts from the last couple of days. I need access to the NSA's satellites."

I hung up the phone and then turned back to Adri who was watching me with a frown on her face. "It was Rachel, wasn't it?"

"I suspect so. I don't know how she managed it, but I'm almost sure it was her."

Whatever Adri was about to say in response was cut off by Jasmin stomping into my room. "We need to talk."

My beast didn't like her tone, and I was inclined to agree with him. I opened my mouth to tear into her, but the memory of Rachel's note stopped me. Rachel had said that I needed to go easy on Jasmin, and while Rach wasn't omniscient, she knew our pack dynamic as well as anyone else and the fact that she stood outside of the power struggles meant that sometimes she saw things that I missed. Instead of dressing Jasmin down I waved her to a chair.

"Report."

"Isn't that Grayson's job?"

"Yes, yes, it is. He's not here yet though and you are, so you get to be debriefed in his place."

She was still mad, but she'd come expecting a fight and my response had thrown her off balance.

"It was the scariest thing I've ever seen. We got inside the building without any problems. Ash shot both of the desk guards with a tranquilizer gun before they could react and then we searched the place floor by floor. There was a basement five levels underground that had almost two dozen caged werewolves in it."

"They changed when they saw you?"

"Yeah, they changed and then went at their cages like there was no tomorrow. Killing them inside of the cages was tricky. Ash burned through two whole clips from his assault rifle killing just one of them so the hybrids started surrounding a few cages at a time and bleeding them out through the bars."

Jasmin took a deep breath and then lifted her shirt up far enough for me to see the huge swaths of gauze and tape that had been used to keep her from bleeding to death.

"Everything was going pretty well right up until all of the cages opened up automatically and the remaining vacuums tried to swarm us under."

"Grayson said that you guys didn't lose anyone."

She looked away for a moment and when she turned back to me her eyes were full of challenge once again.

"We didn't lose anyone, but it was a close thing. Almost everyone took at least one serious wound and I nearly didn't make it out of there alive."

This was what was bothering her, but I knew Jasmin well enough to be certain that she wasn't pissed about something as trivial as a fight that just hadn't gone as well as she would have liked.

"What happened, Jas?"

"I reached out for my beast and tried to transform and she didn't react. I jumped away, still on two legs, and took almost enough damage to kill me. It wasn't until I was bleeding on the floor that my beast finally responded and transformed."

"I'm glad you survived the fight, Jasmin, but those wounds don't look as bad as you're indicating that they were."

"They healed when I transformed. Not the normal amount either, they healed a lot."

"Interesting, that doesn't seem to gel with your problem transforming."

"No, no, it doesn't. I don't know what's going on, Alec, but I suspect that you're the cause of all of this and I don't appreciate it."

She'd gone from calm and rational to angry and moving into my personal space like someone had flipped a switch inside of her. I put a hand up and stopped her from getting any closer.

"Is that your beast driving things now, Jas?"

She suddenly looked lost. "Yes, she just surged up when I thought about the fact that you're sucking me dry, that this is all your fault and you don't even seem sorry."

My beast didn't like how aggressive she was being but I forced him down and gave her a sad smile.

"I'm sorry that you're suffering. I'll keep you out of combat ops until we figure all of this out. I'm keeping a tight leash on my ability right now, I have been keeping it under control for weeks now, but you're right. Anything odd with your beast right now is probably a side effect from before when I was unconsciously draining you. I'm sorry, Jas. I wish I could go back and do a lot of things differently."

She'd been expecting a fight and she didn't know how to handle an apology. I breathed a sigh of relief that I wasn't going to have to beat Jasmin down while Adri watched. My sigh made Jasmin cock her head slightly to the side in puzzlement, but before she could say anything a series of loud beeps sounded from underneath my bed.

It was a digital recorder of some kind and it clicked over to Rachel's voice as I was still fishing it out from under my bed.

"I'm glad that I get one more chance to speak to the three of you. You're three of the most important people in my life and it's only fitting that you're all in one place right now. Your attack on his werewolves in Salt Lake forced Puppeteer's hand. He originally had two forces, which would have been more than enough to kill us all, but you have a chance against what is left. They'll hit the estate sometime in the next few seconds and they'll start with the corner nearest to Ben's room."

I looked up, but Jasmin was already disappearing into the hall. I grabbed the radio sitting on the desk with my computer and depressed the transmit button.

"We're about to be attacked. I want everyone at the garages right now."

My order was just short enough to fit perfectly in the pause that Rachel had left in the recording.

"You're not ready to go head to head with Puppeteer, Alec. You're going to need to split up your people, whoever survives this attack. Jasmin, Jess, Ash, they all have things that they need to go do. The three will go their separate ways, two by their own decision, one because he no longer has a choice."

There was a pause for several seconds. I half thought that Rachel's message was over, but there was a quiet hum in the background of the recording that told me she had something else to say.

"I'm really going to miss the two of you. The light burns my eyes, but the darkness is growing."

There was a sing-song quality to the last bit of what she'd said. I turned to ask Adri what she thought when the first werewolf came crashing through my window.

Chapter 24

Jasmin Bianchi
Graves Estate
Sanctuary, Utah

I raced through the house with every ounce of speed I could muster until I reached the other wing, at which point I was forced to dodge the flow of people headed the other direction. I was only a dozen feet from Ben's room when I heard the first impact as a werewolf crashed through one of the huge, floor-to-ceiling windows that almost every room in this wing sported.

I made it into Ben's room as a second werewolf crashed into the house, this one taking out another window and part of the wall less than twenty feet away from Ben. The lights went out and the machinery around Ben's bed instantly started beeping to alert whoever was listening to the fact that they'd lost power.

Adrenaline already had my heart racing, but I felt another wave hit as I realized how hopeless our situation was. There was a chance that I could outrun the creature, but I wasn't going to abandon Ben to it, which meant that I wasn't going to make it out of the room alive.

A part of me wanted to despair, but mostly I was just mad. I'd spent years trying to get Ben to open up to me. I'd been thwarted at every turn, but up until now I'd always felt like there was still a chance for things to work out.

It was a minor thing compared to everything else the Coun'hij had done, but I was about to lose everything on the altar of their ambition.

It didn't much matter whether I fought the werewolf on two legs or four. I'd die just the same in either form, but I didn't have it in me to just passively wait for it to kill me. Mindful of my difficulties transforming earlier that evening, I reached for my beast with all of the rage I could muster and felt the change rip through me with a level of violence and power that I hadn't realized was possible.

For a split second that seemed to last forever I felt sharp stabs of pain as my bones were forced into new shapes, shapes that they'd never been meant to hold. It was just like the first few times I'd transformed, back before habit and exposure had desensitized me to the agony. I stumbled slightly and then shook my head as I stepped forward.

I was on my second step before I realized that I was still on two legs rather than four. Everything was wrong, my point of view was too high to be a wolf and my nose wasn't sensitive enough. Alec had caused my body to fail me again. I opened my mouth and the scream of rage that escaped was wrong too. My voice was deeper, almost alien in timber.

I was between Ben and the werewolf so I looked down for a split second and took in the massive, *hybrid* body that had replaced my normal form.

A flicker of movement was the only warning I got. I threw myself forward, desperate to intercept the werewolf before it got to Ben.

I was fast, much faster than I'd been as a wolf lately, but the werewolf was even faster and I didn't have any of the right kind of reflexes for this fight.

I hit the werewolf with all of the force I could muster, clipping it on the left side as I drove the talons on my right hand into its chest. The answering blow from the werewolf opened up the right side of my back but I succeeded, against all odds, in knocking it to the ground.

I latched onto its arm with my fangs and left arm, and then tried to use my grip on its chest to control it, but it seemed unfazed by the pain and it was simply too strong for me to control by brute force.

I felt bright ribbons of pain tear through me as its fangs latched onto my shoulder and then our positions were reversed and it was on top of me. There was noise from out in the hall, but I was too concentrated on the wicked, double-edged claws slowly descending towards my throat to worry about anything that far away. I got both legs up so that they were between the werewolf and me, but it wasn't enough to do more than just slightly slow its progress. I was still only seconds from having my throat ripped out.

James came out of nowhere, hitting the werewolf in a blur of motion that pulled its claws back away from me without actually managing to bowl it over.

The werewolf used the force of James' attack to rock back on its feet, lifting me with one hand in an almost unimaginable display of strength as James fought to keep its left arm immobilized. With my right shoulder still being ground to pieces by the creature's fangs, I wasn't in any position to use my right arm, but I sank my feet talons in even deeper and pushed in an effort to keep it from bringing its right arm around to savage James.

It was a poor kind of stalemate, one that could only last a few seconds until blood loss weakened me too much to continue the fight, but Dominic hit the werewolf a second later as it spun around to drive James into a wall.

Dom was incredibly small against the vast bulk of the werewolf, but she clawed her way up its back nearly to its neck before it threw itself backwards, impaling her on a broken two-by-four from where it had come through the exterior wall.

We hit so hard that the sliver of wood was pushed all the way through Dominic and into the werewolf.

Dominic let out a low hiss of pain as the werewolf started to pull itself off of the improvised spear, and then suddenly a slender figure stepped into my view and put a pistol up against the werewolf's head.

Three shots rang out in less than a second and then we all collapsed into a bloody heap as the werewolf's jaws finally relaxed and released my shoulder. A second later Kristin was trying to pull me back to my feet.

"We've got to get it off of Dom or she'll suffocate."

James had taken a pretty good beating too, but he was in better shape than I was, so once I'd managed to roll out of the way, he and Kristin pushed the dead werewolf off of Dom. As James pulled Dom off of the two-by-four she convulsed and then melted back into her normal shape.

The change slowed the bleeding, but we needed to get her to Donovan soon or she wouldn't make it. Kristin didn't waste any time unhooking Ben's IV.

"I don't know where Jasmin is, but we need to get Ben out of here right now or she'll never see him again."

I found that my voice was working again. "How did you know to come help us?"

"I've spent the last hour or so reliving this attack again and again. Dream Stealer shoved me into some kind of endless loop and kept me there until after the attack started so that I couldn't warn anyone."

Kristin finished disconnecting Ben from the machinery around his bed and then motioned me over. "Look, I don't know who you are, but can you at least pick him up and help carrying him out? If Jasmin's not here then she's either dead or hurt somewhere and we don't have very long to find her."

James' chuckle was darkly humorous. "Let me make introductions. Kristin, this is the new and improved Jasmin. Don't piss her off; her bite just got a whole lot worse than her bark."

Chapter 25

Jessica Engel
Graves Estate
Sanctuary, Utah

Wyatt had just returned from Salt Lake and the attack interrupted a truly spectacular fight. One second Wyatt and I were yelling at each other in a way that we both knew would lead to an equally amazing make out session and the next thing I knew Carson had charged into Wyatt's room.

"Alec just announced that an attack is imminent, we need to get you both to the garage!"

Somehow I hadn't believed that we could really be attacked, not now that Alec had so many shape shifters here at the estate. I was so shocked that I followed Wyatt and Carson nearly a dozen steps down the hall before I remembered Andrew.

"Wait, I need to get my dad! He probably doesn't even know that we're under attack."

Wyatt didn't hesitate, turning back towards me, but Carson grabbed his shoulder.

"We can't risk it. I'll send Grayson to get him, but you're too important to be running around like this. If Puppeteer has sent a couple dozen werewolves they'll kill almost everyone here before Alec even gets his people organized."

For all that I'd been thinking just a moment before that an attack was impossible, there was something about Carson's statement that rang true. He was right; anyone not at the garage by the time the attack got here was probably going to die.

For a split second I almost started back down the hall towards them. Andrew was my father, but he was also the next best thing to a stranger. A few months of awkward conversations wasn't enough to create a real family bond and I was the most scared I'd been since the last werewolf fight I'd been in.

The fear was incredibly real, it had me shaking, but I set all of that aside and shook my head. "I'm not leaving it to Grayson, who knows if he's even as close as we are to my dad's room. I'm going."

As I turned and headed the other direction, I saw Wyatt remove Carson's hand from his shoulder and start towards me.

The house was a complete zoo. People I barely knew were running everywhere, some trying to get to the garage, some trying to make sure a loved one was safe. We were still thirty seconds away from Andrew's room when I heard the first few werewolves enter the house. Between the sound of walls buckling and the screams from people who hadn't made it far enough away in time, it was impossible to miss the arrival of the creatures that'd been sent to kill us.

This wing of the house had a series of large open rooms that each of the bedrooms opened off of. Andrew met us just outside his room in the open area where he and I had spent so many hours over the last few months trying to get reacquainted. His face was white and I suddenly realized that he was more worried about me than he was himself. I got only a glimpse of his expression before the lights went out, plunging the entire room into darkness.

There was another crash, this time from the direction of Andrew's room, and Wyatt and Carson transformed in a roar of power as they stepped between Andrew and whatever was in his room. A second later Grayson appeared out of the room, but my momentary relief at seeing him was quickly soured by the expression on his face.

"We need to move. I heard two of them coming around the corner of the house just before I ducked into Andrew's room."

I grabbed the back of Andrew's wheelchair and started pushing him back the way we'd just come. Carson slipped by me and took point as

Wyatt and Grayson caught up to us. Before we'd even made it all of the way through the next open space, another crash sounded behind us and Grayson swore.

"Keep moving, I'll try to delay it."

I pushed harder, trying to squeeze a little more speed out of my tired body, but Andrew's chair wasn't really built for speed and my two-legged form wasn't much better. We dodged around an artfully laid out loveseat and couch and then I heard the one sound that was guaranteed to make our escape impossible.

There was another crash, this one coming from ahead of us, and then I heard the heavy footprints of another werewolf stalking back towards us as its dark, earthy scent preceded it. Grayson swore again and then I heard him pushing Wyatt ahead of him.

"It's the one I smelled a couple of seconds ago. Puppeteer is controlling them, maybe not completely, but enough to trap us."

Carson didn't say anything, he just grunted and charged the werewolf ahead of us. It was a long shot, but I figured that if I could help Carson keep the werewolf occupied that there was a chance that Andrew could slip past it.

I abandoned Andrew's chair and jumped forward, letting a transformation explode out of me while I was still in midair without bothering to strip out of my clothes first. I hit the ground with all four feet underneath me, and sprang towards Carson, hoping the whole time that I'd get there in time.

Before that instant I would have said that there wasn't any single hybrid who could stand up to a werewolf, even a small one, and live. Seeing Carson in action I suddenly realized that, while he wasn't quite the werewolf's match, he was closer than I ever would have believed was possible.

Carson moved forward in jerky fits and starts, slashing the werewolf's arms before ducking backwards to avoid its ripostes. It wasn't until I was mid-leap that I realized that there was a method to his retreats. He'd always backed away to the left, which meant he'd gradually turned the werewolf around, which was the only reason that I had even a tiny chance of landing my current lunge towards the werewolf's flank.

The werewolf whirled around, almost faster than I could follow, but I managed to get a piece of its left arm. Its right arm came around in a blur to scrape me off, but Carson stepped in closer and sank his claws into its arm. It wasn't a disabling attack, in fact it barely even slowed the werewolf down, but that fraction of a second was all I needed to relax my jaws slightly so that the werewolf's own spin knocked me free, but not before I'd ripped a healthy chunk of flesh out of its triceps.

Despite the failing lights, I caught a flash of the other fight as I sailed through the air, and it didn't look good. The other vacuum had both Wyatt and Grayson on the defensive and while it was bleeding from a couple of pretty good slashes, both of them were bleeding even more profusely.

I hit the wall hard enough that I saw stars, but I managed to land right side up and I spun around just in time to see Carson take a wicked blow to the right side of his chest. My follow-up spring bought Carson enough time to dart back out of range, but it was obvious to me that we didn't have much longer.

I didn't manage to put teeth on the werewolf this time, and it raked a claw along my side as I tried to evade its follow-up attack. Carson attacked again, this time ducking under a swipe and then lunging forward, sinking his talons into the werewolf's legs. Carson scaled the werewolf, climbing up it like some kind of massive, moving tree, but he'd mistimed his initial move and he didn't make it far enough around. Werewolves had the same weakness to attacks from behind that hybrids had, but Carson was far enough out of position that the werewolf was able to connect with its elbow as it threw itself back into one of the large marble columns that helped support the vaulted ceiling.

I heard Carson's ribs break from more than a dozen feet away. He lost his hold on the werewolf and dropped to the ground as I tried to get in and latch onto something vital for the third time.

Carson yelled out in pain as I managed to tear another chunk of muscle out of the back of the werewolf's left leg. Carson rolled back to his feet, but there was a hitch to his movements that told me some of the ribs had separated and were digging into his lungs. The werewolf's backfist was more fist than claws, but it still sent me tumbling head over paws into a couch that was nearly destroyed in the process.

Carson didn't instantly dart in for another exchange and the werewolf seemed happy to catch its breath as well. As I pulled myself back to my feet I noticed a stabbing pain every time I breathed. None of us had made it through the last minute or so unscathed, but the werewolf was winning by points. It was just too massive and tough. It would kill us long before we'd manage to wear it down enough to create the kind of opening we'd need to end the fight.

Carson circled slightly and the werewolf honored the greater threat he represented by turning slightly so that it still faced him, but I knew it didn't really matter. Our opponent was just too fast for me to get inside its defenses.

Carson's expression changed slightly, his broad face settled into something that I thought was calm, but I wasn't sure. It was so rare to see a hybrid in a state of peace that I could have been mistaken, but a second later Carson threw himself at the werewolf in an explosion of violence that brought it down onto one knee. He hit the leg I'd injured earlier with both sets of talons, and then grabbed onto its left arm with his claws and fangs.

It was the perfect setup for me and I took it with reflexes that I'd finally buckled down and spent the last two months rewiring. I sailed through the air in what felt like slow motion, expecting the whole time that the werewolf would shrug Carson off and then rip me out of the air, but it didn't happen. Carson kept hold of the werewolf despite the claws that were turning his chest into gruesome ribbons.

A split second later my jaws latched onto the werewolf's neck and I hit hard enough and at just the right angle to snap its neck.

It was unprecedented, and I felt a flush of pride wash through me right up until I realized that Carson wasn't pulling himself back to his feet. I heard a scream of rage and loss and then turned just in time to see Wyatt throw himself at the second werewolf.

It was almost like Grayson was anticipating Wyatt's suicidal attack. The massive hybrid stepped in, taking a nasty set of slashes across his shoulder as he sank his claws into the werewolf's throat.

A second later the werewolf was collapsing in a spray of blood and Grayson was dragging Wyatt back out of range of its death throes. Andrew was next to me, somehow having managed not to be taken out by the flying debris.

"Check on Carson, I'll keep moving forward while you guys triage."

I stumbled over to Carson, melting back into my normal form as I went. Carson had abandoned his hybrid shape as well, a reflexive, last-ditch attempt by his body to heal the damage and keep him alive, but I could tell even without checking his pulse that he wasn't going to make it.

His face was still calm, but he pulled me down to my knees with surprising strength so that he could whisper into my ear.

"You have to keep Wyatt alive. Everything depends on it now. Be patient with him, eventually he'll tell you the truth, he's too good of a man to do otherwise."

I watched the light go out of Carson's eyes and then stumbled back to my feet, wading through wreckage and blood motivated only by the hope that Wyatt's injuries weren't likewise fatal.

Chapter 26

'Ash' Hunt
Graves Estate
Sanctuary, Utah

The various lights scattered about the estate, some working, some not, gave the landscape an unearthly feel. The lights that were still working flickered occasionally, sometimes because of a nearby werewolf, sometimes just because of the sheer damage that had been done to the manor house.

A dull red glow gave lie to the idea that portions of the house might be saved still. We didn't have the manpower to fight a fire, not while we still had to worry about an attack from the Coun'hij at any moment. Firefighters were out of the question as well. Alec had gone silent just after the attack started, but I knew he wouldn't want to expose any more innocents to harm than we absolutely had to.

RIVEN

There weren't many people who would be able to watch thousands of years of history go up in flames, taking with them the multimillion-dollar structure that had housed them, and not feel compelled to do something to save it all, but for Alec money really had been...was...just a tool.

I saw hulking figures approaching through the near darkness and I flipped the selector on my rifle to full-auto. It was probably Isaac and the others that I'd sent back into the house for survivors, but I couldn't be sure, not at this range, not with the breeze blowing their direction. Besides, if Alec wasn't with them, then my authority was going to evaporate like so much smoke.

I'd have given responsibility for this mess over to someone else in a heartbeat if I'd thought that they had a prayer of getting us all out alive, but the pack leaders were either missing or injured and the rest of the survivors weren't likely to do any better than me when it came to keeping everyone in one piece.

If I had to shoot Isaac to keep everyone else in line then I'd do it and deal with the consequences and regret later.

Less than a minute later the figures had gotten close enough to confirm that it was Isaac and the others and I relaxed slightly. Every one of them was bloodied and obviously exhausted, but he hadn't lost anyone and it looked like they'd found some survivors. I waited until they were close enough that we stood a chance of not being overheard before I spoke.

"Report."

Isaac gave me a surly look, but he gestured back at the main structure of the house. "There isn't anyone else alive back there. We ran into one more werewolf in there. I think that Puppeteer forgot about it or was busy with other stuff because it was just destroying the house randomly rather than actively hunting for survivors."

"You guys put it down?"

"Yeah, but it was a close thing."

"Who'd you find?"

Brutus and Arnold had reached us now, but the extent of the injuries to the two forms they were carrying made it hard to say for sure who they'd dragged out of the building just moments before the fire would have consumed them.

"Rex and Jane."

Arnold shook his head as he cradled the smaller figure in his arms. "Jane didn't make it, she died five minutes ago, but I couldn't bear to just leave her in there."

Jane was just one casualty among many, but I still swayed slightly on my feet. She'd never even had a chance. Most of the dead were submissives or noncombatants who hadn't managed to find help before the werewolves had found them. It was too easy to see myself or

Kristin in the bodies that were lined up on one side of the driveway.

I forced myself to concentrate on the living and turned to Brutus. "Donovan and Mallory are still working on the injured. Please take Rex into the garage and help Donovan. Hopefully you guys found him in time."

Isaac waited until Brutus and Arnold left and then stepped into my personal space, his voice low and menacing. "Alec hasn't shown up yet, has he?"

"No, he hasn't, but that doesn't mean that he's dead."

"Yes, it does. We looked through the whole damn house and there are bodies everywhere in there. I don't even know half of the people who died tonight, but there was no sign of Alec. I held out hope until we made it to his room. That's where the fire started, but it looked like the roof collapsed long before the fire started weakening the structure. My bet is that Puppeteer made sure to take him out at the very start of the attack."

"That doesn't make sense. The werewolves clearly hit the section of the house with Ben in it first. That's clear on the other side of things from Alec's room."

"Maybe it was all a giant ruse to concentrate the resistance on that side of the house so that he could sneak a kill team into Alec's room. All I know is that Alec isn't here and that means that I don't have to take orders from you."

I let the muzzle of my rifle rise slightly as I gave Isaac my best blank face. "You really want to do this right now? We've got bodies in the house, more bodies in the garage, and nobody who's still alive is unwounded. Based on what the lights are doing out there, we still have werewolves in the area and unless the Coun'hij has all become a bunch of idiots they have a bunch of their enforcers en route to mop up whoever the werewolves don't tear through. Do you really want to rock the boat right now?"

"I'm dominant to you."

"Yes, yes, you are. You're not dominant enough though to survive a chest full of five seven rounds and if that's what it takes to carry out Alec's order to assemble everyone here and keep them safe then that's what I'll do, Isaac."

Our standoff stretched out for several seconds until movement off to our right brought both of us around. The smoke was even worse than it had been before and it almost made me doubt what I was seeing.

Alec stepped out of the darkness with his mother clasped in his arms and Adri trailing along behind him. All three of them looked like they'd been through hell, but Alec was covered in blood. That wasn't the most incredible thing though. The thing that positively blew my mind was the unearthly light coming off of their skin. I knew it was only my moonborn eyes that allowed me to see anything, but I'd never seen anyone glow that brightly, let alone two humans.

Alec took in the tension between Isaac and me and then handed his mother off to Isaac. "Please report, Ash."

Isaac looked for a moment like he was going to protest, but Alec turned pale blue eyes that were only a hairsbreadth from transforming on him and Isaac finally nodded and headed towards the garage.

"It's a relief to see you."

"You too, now tell me what's going on."

"We've got all of the survivors gathered here inside and around the garage. Isaac just took a team back through the house and it wasn't pretty. We've lost a lot of people."

Alec closed his eyes for a moment and then nodded. "I figured as much. It was unavoidable considering how little warning we had and the fact that most of the fighters had already been through the wringer once tonight."

We stood in silence for nearly a minute before Adri wrapped her arms around Alec and whispered into his ear. She probably meant for it to be inaudible to anyone other than Alec but I was close enough to hear her.

"Concentrate on the living. Your mom and Rachel are both still alive and we couldn't have done anything different than we did."

Alec nodded and then looked back at me. "Did Grayson make it out alive?"

"Yeah. He got beat up pretty good, but he's alive still. He won't leave Wyatt's side though. Carson was killed in the fighting and it doesn't look like Wyatt will make it."

Alec flinched a little at Adri's gasp, but he just stroked her hand and nodded. "Go get Grayson and as many effectives as we still have. We only have a couple of minutes before they come for us."

I paused midway through turning to carry out his order. "How do you know?"

"I can feel them out there, all of them."

I didn't understand, not really, but I nodded and double-timed it into the garage. Things were even worse than I'd remembered from the last time I'd been inside our 'sanctuary.' Wounded were on almost every open inch of the concrete, blood soaking through bandages, their breathing labored.

Donovan was working on Wyatt while Mallory played nurse, but I could see defeat in every line of his posture. I stepped into Grayson's field of vision and pointed outside. "Alec is back and he needs you outside."

"I'm not leaving Wyatt."

I pressed my rifle into his chest and gave him a cold smile. "You swore an oath. If you use your power on me now the convulsions will make my finger tighten on the trigger. Get out there before Alec has to come in here and get you himself."

I'd just made an enemy, but he nodded and slowly backed away from me. I watched him leave out the side door and then turned to find that Jasmin had come over to see what all of the fuss was about.

She'd pulled a ha'bit on, probably from one of the RV's, but that wasn't the only thing different about her. Even with all we'd been through in the last hour or so, the rumor mill was still working and everyone here knew that she'd manifested a hybrid shape well after such a thing should have been impossible.

The piece that hadn't made the rounds yet was just how big her hybrid form was. Kristin had quietly told me that Jasmin was the largest hybrid she'd ever seen, that she towered over James and was nearly the size of one of the smaller, younger werewolves.

"What's up, Ash?"

"Alec just arrived. He says that we're due for another attack and wants me to gather everyone that can still fight."

"Don't worry about it. I'll go round everyone up and meet you outside in a minute. You don't need to be pissing anyone else off today."

There was the rub. Right now Jasmin wasn't any more dangerous than I was, but she was a hybrid now. Unless someone killed her over the next couple of months she'd grow into the potential of her new form and then she'd be the next best thing to unstoppable.

I nodded and walked back outside just in time to see Alec gently send Adri into the garage. Once it was just the three of us, Alec turned to Grayson and pointed off to the east. "They're clustered out there. When I give you the signal I want you to use your power to immobilize the northern half of the attacking force."

Grayson shook his head tiredly. "My power won't work on werewolves. Even if there are shape shifters with them the werewolves will still short-circuit my ability. I'm no more valuable to you right now than any other hybrid."

Alec's smile was as unworried as I'd ever seen out of him. "You just act on my signal and leave the werewolves to me."

Jasmin walked out a couple of seconds later followed by a battered string of men and women who were the best we had left to offer up to the gods of battle.

Alec looked them over, the strange glow from a few minutes before mostly gone, and gave them all a sad smile. "Thank you. I know that each of you has probably lost someone tonight. I'm sorry to ask you to step up once again, but we have one last battle tonight before we can stop and nurse our wounds."

There was a low, unhappy murmur, but a sudden gesture from Alec stopped it. "I want you to look around right now. Take in the faces of those next to you and remember them. You're all witnesses. After tonight nothing will ever be the same again. You'll be different; each of you will be something more than you are right now. After tonight you are all *truly* mine."

Silence reigned supreme for a handful of heartbeats and then the sound of taloned feet brought us all around.

Alec unconcernedly stepped out in front of us as the first of the werewolves appeared out of the smoke, running towards us with the inexorability of time. The half-dozen werewolves were flanked by the better part of thirty shape shifters and I felt my heart drop. Even if we could somehow defeat the werewolves, we wouldn't be a match for the Coun'hij's bully boys.

I pulled my rifle up and sighted on the lead werewolf, waiting for it to close the distance slightly as my finger started to tighten down on the trigger.

In the split second before my first shot rang out, Alec lit up even more brightly than he'd been when he'd first arrived.

The enemy line disintegrated into a sudden melee as most of the werewolves instantly turned on the shape shifters flanking them. I felt a surge of euphoria at the sight of our opponents tearing each other to shreds, but even then I knew it was too much to hope that they'd kill each other to a man.

The fight was brief but brutal and five seconds later the werewolves had all been cut down and the shape shifters had lost a third of their number. It took a few seconds for the Coun'hij enforcers to shake back out into a loose line, but then they once again started towards us, confident in their greater numbers.

Alec waited until they were only fifteen yards away from us before tapping Grayson on the arm. Grayson immobilized half of the opposing force while Alec dropped the other half. The fight was over less than a minute later and Alec was right. With one fight we had changed everything and every single one of us belonged to him in ways that we didn't fully understand.

Chapter 27

Adriana Paige
Graves Estate
Sanctuary, Utah

I spent another terrified fifteen minutes inside the garage waiting for the werewolves to overrun Alec and the rest. I knew what I'd seen when we went to save Alec's mother, but it still seemed too unreal for me to believe that Alec would be able to turn the tide of the fight.

My fear for Alec and the rest was strong enough to cushion me from the horror around me right up until I heard a cheer of celebration break out from just outside the garage. Once I knew we were safe, I looked at my surroundings and felt a wave of near despair wash over me. There were so many people who were on death's doorstep.

I found Dominic first and nearly cried at the massive hole in her stomach that someone had tried to cover up with gauze. I picked her hand up and felt my hopes fall even further at just how cold she was. Shape shifters could maintain their body heat in almost any environment. For Dominic to be this cold she had to be hurt badly enough that even her natural regenerative abilities weren't working any more.

I sat there holding Dom's hand and finally let all of the tears out. Tears for Carson, tears for Dom, tears even for Rachel who was probably still alive but out there in a world she no longer understood without anyone to watch out for her.

As my tears splashed onto Dom's hand I realized that something had changed. Her skin wasn't just warming up because I was holding her, it was heating up on its own with a rapidity that was impossible. It had to be some kind of flash fever. I was looking around for someone I could ask for help from when Dom tugged on my hand.

"Where am I, Adri? What happened?"

"You're in the garage, there was an attack and you were hurt."

She looked up at me with curiosity in her eyes. "I remember the fight to save Ben, I remember being stabbed, but I feel fine."

Before I could stop her she pulled off the gauze that had been the only thing keeping her from bleeding to death. I went to grab the bloody material and put it back on her stomach but there was no need. She wiped the dried blood away and underneath there was nothing but a perfect expanse of unbroken skin.

"It's finally working again."

"What do you mean, Dom?"

She ignored my question and pulled herself to her feet. "Who's hurt the worst?"

None of it made any sense, but after what I'd seen Alec do earlier it was hard to deny that anything was possible. I helped Dominic over to Rex, who had a series of bandages across his head and chest, yelling the entire time for Donovan.

I watched as Rex's color visibly improved and then Dominic was blindly reaching for me again. Her eyes remained closed as I led her over to Rebekka and by the time Rebekka's breathing had normalized Donovan was there to help guide Dom.

We were an odd procession, Donovan, Dominic and I followed by those who Dominic had healed, but we made our slow, steadily weakening way through the garage and then just when I didn't think that Dominic could continue, Alec arrived and placed his hands on Dominic's shoulders.

I still didn't have any explanation for what was happening, but I caught the very fringe of what Alec did to Dominic and it was like he washed away all of my pain and exhaustion. I suddenly felt like I'd just rolled out of bed after the best night's sleep ever.

Sheer chance had put Wyatt in the corner of the garage farthest from where Dom and I had started, and by the time we worked our way through everyone else Dom was stumbling and exhausted again.

She collapsed on the floor next to Wyatt and put her hands over his chest. I felt his skin heat up even from several inches away as he almost seemed to go into convulsions. A few seconds later he collapsed back down onto the concrete and Jessica frantically started unwrapping bandages.

Wyatt's chest was unmarred again except for the odd circular scar that we'd noticed shortly after he'd arrived in Sanctuary. I didn't think anything of it necessarily until I realized that Donovan hadn't been limping for the last fifteen minutes that he'd been helping Dominic.

"Donovan, I'm sorry if this is inappropriate, but could you please lift your pant leg?"

I received odd looks from everyone, Donovan included, but then I saw the same realization dawn in his eyes that I'd just experienced. Donovan slowly rolled one side of his pants up to his knee and there wasn't a single trace of scar tissue.

Chapter 28

Adriana Paige
I-80
Northern Nevada

We'd all wanted to sit there and revel in the miracle of Dominic's healing powers, but Alec had cajoled everyone into vehicles and got our huge convoy moving away from the estate.

I spent the first leg of our journey crying over all of the people that we'd lost. Some of them had already started to get fuzzy inside my mind, almost as though I was subconsciously trying to shield myself from the pain of our losses, but my mental picture of Carson was still incredibly vivid.

I wanted to stay curled up in a ball in the back bedroom, but once the initial rush of tears passed, my mind started playing back Carson's advice from the last time we'd been in the park together.

I knew I needed to pull myself together and start exercising the influence I did have to help keep everything together. It wouldn't be fair to just leave that entirely on Alec's shoulders. It was hard to talk to Alec with everyone else around and I spent a little while worrying that Alec was going to keep everyone together rather than dispersing us as Rachel had warned in her recording, but Alec addressed that point once we stopped in Nevada at a tiny rest stop. Alec asked for Grayson and Wyatt as soon as our massive RV stopped moving. Predictably Jess arrived trailing along behind Wyatt.

"Your oaths to me are at the point of expiring. What are your plans?"

Grayson didn't say anything, instead looking at Wyatt like the younger man was in charge.

"I'm not sure. I...I need some time to process Carson's death, so I'll be leaving for a while, but I think that maybe it's almost time for you to meet someone."

"Who?"

"I can't tell you, not really. All I can say is that he's the one who started all of this and that I'm finally starting to understand why Carson was so adamant that the two of you need to meet."

I could tell that Alec wasn't satisfied with the answer, but he also didn't seem willing to push Wyatt right now, not when it meant risking alienating Grayson.

"The two of you will both be leaving then?"

This time it was Grayson who nodded. "The three of us left together, it is my duty to finish the journey with Wyatt. Carson would have done the same had he any choice."

I suddenly felt as though I'd been slapped as I realized that Rachel's cryptic warning about 'the three' was the second time I'd heard that reference. I grabbed Alec before he could respond to Grayson.

"Rachel's warning. The last bit about the three, that wasn't talking about Jasmin, Jess and Ash, it was talking about Carson, Wyatt and Grayson. They need to go their separate ways, two of them because they have a choice, the third because he no longer has any choices."

Alec considered my words for a moment and then nodded. "Rachel left a recording warning us of the attack last night. I've spent hours trying to figure out how she knew, but I'm sure that she wasn't working with Puppeteer and the rest. All I can assume is that she's got a precognitive feeding her hints about the future. Possibly Adri's priest. I think we should follow her advice in this instance. Grayson, I'd like you to swear fealty for another two months and accompany Tasha. I promised to keep her safe and you represent the best odds of making that happen."

Wyatt considered the request for nearly a minute before nodding. "I won't need your help where I'm going, Grayson. You can stay if you'd like."

The rest of the day was more of the same as Alec carefully split his people up into small teams that were to be scattered about the country.

Jasmin was taking Ben to look for someone who could cure him. Dominic had tried and while his breathing and pulse had strengthened slightly, he hadn't woken up.

For reasons I don't think he even understood, Alec teamed Isaac up with Kristin and Ash. James and Dominic were temporarily going to take care of Addison, Andrew, and Alec's mom, while Donovan and Mallory would be coming with us.

Dozens of other people filtered through the RV, some I recognized and some who were too new for me to have learned their names yet, but mostly I just felt the holes left by those who'd fallen in the fight to defend the manor.

Donovan, Mallory, Alec and I stood and watched the last vehicle drive away as the sun started dipping down towards the horizon. Grayson and Tasha were the last to leave, mostly because Tasha had fought her assignment.

As their car disappeared onto the interstate Mallory sighed. "Poor Grayson."

Alec chuckled. "Tasha is a handful, but she's not *that* bad."

"I wasn't thinking of Tasha. That man bears a terrible burden and I shudder to think what will be demanded of him before all is said and done."

Alec's levity disappeared instantly. "What do you mean?"

"No, Alec. I've said too much already. I make it a policy to never discuss certain of the things I see, not even with you."

I could see Alec debating whether or not to press her, but Dominic had spent some time healing the worst of Mallory's scars and regaining a measure of her health had made her even more determined than ever.

"Fine, the next time you see Grayson discuss it with him. I'd like to know what you're talking about so I don't add to his burden needlessly. For now, I suppose I should get used to the unexpected. Between Jasmin manifesting a hybrid form and Dominic becoming a healer, I feel like we've used up our store of miracles for the foreseeable future. Let's get inside and back on the road. I'll drive so that Donovan can continue to work on spinning the disaster back at the estate."

Donovan smiled. He looked younger than he'd been even just a few days ago. "I'm happy to report that I have the work there well in hand. I must say, Master Alec, that pressing for the construction of that nuclear power plant just outside of town was a stroke of genius. I think we'll safely be able to blame everything on an accident there. We already have several teams there doing damage control with the police and fire department."

Alec smiled. "Thank goodness for miracles small and large."

Once we were back on the road with Alec driving and me in the passenger seat I broached the last thing that had been bothering me since shortly after we'd pulled over at the rest stop.

"About those changes, Alec. I don't think we've seen the last of them, but I also don't think we've properly recognized some of the ones that have already happened."

"What do you mean?"

"I don't think that Rachel is being tipped off by a precognitive, I think *Rachel* is the precognitive. I think she can see the future and I think *that* is what is driving her crazy."

Author's Note

It's always a little hard to know what exactly to say once I get to this point, but as always, I really hope that you enjoyed Riven. 2013 should be a banner production year. Riven was mostly written during December of 2012, but it was finished in 2013, and since then I've also finished a rough draft of the 4th Guadel Chronicles book and I'm currently about two thirds of the way through another book focusing on Geoffrey from *The Greater Darkness*.

I hope you'll continue to come along for the ride as Alec, Adri, Va'del and Jain's stories each start their next chapter, and I hope that you'll help spread the word about my books so that others who haven't found them yet can enjoy them as well.

Lastly, if you haven't signed up for my mailing list please consider going to my blog (deanwrites.com) and doing so. It's the best way to stay abreast of any new releases.

Acknowledgements

All of the usual suspects need thanked, but I definitely need to single out my dedicated core of beta readers. Mom and Dad, Shalese, Matthew, Mark, Mimi and Kim have faithfully read almost everything I've written and provided feedback along the way. These books would be worse without their efforts. Thank you all!

My editors, RJ Locksley and Amy Jirsa-Smith did an exemplary job again, and I'm grateful that they continue to do business with me. Any errors in Riven are almost certainly because this stubborn writer refused to heed one or both of their suggestions regarding a proposed fix.

I owe a big thanks to Obsidian Dawn for brushes used in creating the cover for Riven. You can find Obsidian Dawn at www.obsidiandawn.com.

Finally, I'm grateful to Katie and my daughters, for their support. Katie is a real trooper with her editing and cover help and I'm profoundly thankful that I managed to turn her into a fan so long ago.

About the Author

Dean Murray is a prolific author with dozens of titles across multiple pen names and more than half a million copies of his work currently in circulation.

Dean started reading seriously in the second grade due to a competition and has spent most of the subsequent three decades lost in other people's worlds.

Things worsened, or improved depending on your point of view, when he first started experimenting with writing while finishing up his accounting degree.

These days Dean has a wonderful wife and two lovely daughters to keep him rather more grounded, but the idea of bringing others along with him as he meets interesting new people in universes nobody else has ever seen tends to drag him back to his computer on a fairly regular basis.

Keep up to speed on Dean's latest projects at www.DeanWrites.com.

The Greater Darkenss

Dean writing as Eldon Murphy

Something powerful is stirring in the darkness. Something so ancient that even creatures who've been alive for hundreds of years have long since discounted this new threat as nothing more than myth.

Normal humans will be caught in the crossfire, but then that's always the way of things. Geoffrey has no memory of his past life or any idea how to survive in the violent, dangerous world in which he's trapped. Despite his best efforts, he's about to find himself in the middle of a conflict that threatens to sweep away everything, and everyone he's been fighting so hard to protect.

Frozen Prospects

The invitation to join the secretive Guadel should have been the fulfillment of dreams Va'del didn't even realize he had. When his sponsors are killed in an ambush a short time later, he instead finds his probationary status revoked, and becomes a pawn between various factions inside the Guadel ruling body.

Jain's never known any life but that of a Guadel in training. She'd thought herself reconciled to the idea of a loveless marriage for the good of her people, but meeting Va'del changes everything. Their growing attraction flies against hundreds of years of precedent, but as wide-spread attacks threaten their world, the Guadel have no choice but to use even Jain and Va'del in their fight for survival.

CHET:
Whispers From The Past
By Larry Murray

Meet Charles Tucker, he has spent nearly 30 years living in denial, trying desperately to hide from his past and the events that shattered his heart beyond any possibility of healing. He can't let anyone close, for doing so would open him up to being hurt again, and there's no way he could survive another wounding.

Meet the Saunders family, new to the neighborhood and teetering on the verge of bankruptcy. Mark, the father, talks a good story but is that all he is? His plan could hold the key to reversing his family's financial misfortunes, or it could wipe out everyone involved.

Meet Chet, a battered old '64 Chevy pickup that was there on the night Charles' life imploded. For nearly three decades, he has been locked away in an old barn, safely out of sight if not completely out of mind. For 29 years Charles has blamed the old pickup for the destruction of his life, now he's about to find that the vehicle that destroyed his life might be the key to his healing and a journey of unexpected miracles.